We looked at three more apartments before we found one that Paul thought we could afford. I looked around in horror at the dingy brown walls, ill lit by dirty light bulbs suspended from the ceiling.

"It's horrendous!" I whispered.

"We could fix it up," Paul said cheerily. "It definitely has possibilities. You could whip up some curtains and dig up some old rugs—"

"I don't sew," I said firmly.

What kind of person did he think I was, anyway? The kind who wore little frilly aprons and baked brownies?

Dear Readers:

Thank you for your unflagging interest in First Love From Silhouette. Your many helpful letters have shown us that you have appreciated growing and stretching with us, and that you demand more from your reading than happy endings and conventional love stories. In the months to come we will make sure that our stories go on providing the variety you have come to expect from us. We think you will enjoy our unusual plot twists and unpredictable characters who will surprise and delight you without straying too far from the concerns that are very much part of all our daily lives.

We hope you will continue to share with us your ideas about how to keep our books your very First Loves. We depend on you to keep us on our toes!

Nancy Jackson
Senior Editor
FIRST LOVE FROM SILHOUETTE

PLAYING HOUSE
Jean Simon

First Love from Silhouette

Published by Silhouette Books New York

America's Publisher of Contemporary Romance

SILHOUETTE BOOKS
300 E. 42nd St., New York, N.Y. 10017

ISBN: 0-373-06203-6

First Silhouette Books printing September 1986

America's Publisher of Contemporary Romance

Printed in the U.S.A.

RL 5.4, IL age 11 and up

JEAN SIMON grew up in San Diego, California, and lives in Sioux Rapids, Iowa, with her husband and their combined family of six children—three of his, two of hers and one "theirs." She has been writing since she was twelve and has had more than forty short stories published in national magazines. Her favorite locale for her fiction is California.

Chapter One

I stared down at the piece of paper on my desk and resisted the urge to stand up right there in the middle of class and shout that it was all an awful mistake.

Instead, I slumped down in my seat and contemplated the unfairness of life in general. It was just my luck to be stuck with Paul Ryan for the junior class economics experiment. I didn't even know Paul, even though he sat two seats behind me in Mr. Kirkpatrick's economics class. No one knew him very well. He was a new boy who so far had kept pretty much to himself.

My best friend, Daphne Pepper, turned around in her seat and tried to look at the name on my paper.

"Who'd you get?" she whispered. "*I* got Hank Halloran. Can you believe it? For the past year and a half he's been asking me out and I've been turning him down, and now we're practically thrown together for the whole semester. Did you get Clay?"

"No, I didn't," I told her. I would have been ecstatic if I'd gotten Clay as my partner for this experiment. We'd only had a couple of dates, but he was one of the most popular boys in school and I still couldn't quite believe he was interested in me. This experiment would have been a chance for us to spend a lot of time together and get to know each other better. "I got Paul Ryan," I said with a sigh.

"Who?" Daphne's forehead creased in a frown.

"You know." I looked over my shoulder. "Two seats back. Light brown hair. Kind of a nice smile on the rare occasions he bothers to show it."

"Oh, him." Daphne, loyal friend that she was, looked disappointed for me. Then she brightened. That's just the way Daphne was. Even during the worst times she always managed to see a silver cloud. "At least you're better off than Dot Van Atta. She didn't get anyone at all. She's assigned to be a widow with two children who works as a waitress and barely gets by."

Mr. Kirkpatrick began rapping on the blackboard with his pointer. That was his well-known signal for silence, and the buzz in the classroom gradually stopped as everyone faced the front. I did manage to sneak one look at Clay on the other side of the room, to see if he looked disappointed at not getting me for a partner, but he wasn't looking in my direction.

I wondered whom he'd gotten, and hoped it wasn't Chelsea Fischer, or one of his other ex-girlfriends. Chelsea was the prettiest girl in school. That would be too much for me to take.

"Judging by some of the comments I've overheard in the past few minutes," Mr. K. said when he'd gotten everyone's attention, "you aren't all happy with the choices I've made."

There was a general shifting and murmuring until he held up his hand for silence.

"Believe me," he continued. "I didn't just draw names out of a hat. I picked partners carefully. In some cases I matched you up with someone with whom I thought you would be compatible. Others I deliberately mismatched, to see how you would handle the pressure of such a relationship. Some of you, as you know, don't even have partners.''

Daphne leaned back in her seat and whispered, ''I would have preferred being a widow with eight kids to having Hank as a partner.''

I knew exactly how she felt, because I felt the same way. Let's face it. I knew my hold on Clay was pretty shaky, and I didn't need the competition of his being matched with someone else.

Let me explain why this meant so much to me. You see, I used to be something of a bookworm, and at sixteen I was a year younger than the rest of my classmates. That's because back when I was in elementary school they did some tests on me and decided to skip me ahead a grade. Apparently, they got the idea that I was extra bright or something, and would be better off in a more challenging class.

From what I understand they don't do that anymore. I'm glad they don't, because it was the worst thing that ever happened to me. As far as grades go I've always been able to keep up. That's not the problem. The problem is that I'm sort of small, only five three and a hundred and five pounds, so being the youngest to boot has made it nearly impossible for me to get anyone to take me seriously. I was constantly being

called "kid," and "shorty" and—worst of all—
"little Marcy." At times I felt like the class pet,
rather than an equal.

That's why I was so surprised when Clay first
asked me out. I would have sworn he didn't
know I existed, but one day there he was,
standing beside my locker and asking me if I'd
like to go to a movie.

He was tall and gorgeous and popular, everything I longed to be, and I was so thrilled to be
asked out by him that I lost every shred of sophistication I'd ever possessed and said yes so
enthusiastically that I almost expected him to
cancel out right then and there.

Now, resting my hand on my chin, I looked
over at Clay again. He had dimples so deep that
they showed even when he wasn't smiling, and
his straight blond hair was kept short during
basketball season so that it wouldn't get in his
eyes during an important play.

Maybe I could talk Mr. Kirkpatrick into re-
considering his decision.

He was explaining the rest of the experiment
to the class. "On the first of each month I'll give
you each a certain amount of play money, de-
pending on the income I've allotted you. With
that money you'll have to pay rent, utilities,
groceries, plus about a half dozen other ex-

penses. You'll keep a detailed log of your expenditures, and if you overspend in one area—entertainment, for example—you might not have enough money left for necessities.''

I sighed and looked down at my paper. Paul Ryan was my partner and he had a job that paid fairly well, according to the figures Mr. K. had provided. I also worked, but only part-time because I attended classes three evenings a week. We had no children, thank goodness. I didn't see how we would have any trouble living on the net monthly income Mr. K. had so generously given us. Maybe if things went smoothly enough Paul and I wouldn't actually have to spend much time together on this project.

''You'll have over the weekend to plan apartments or other housing,'' Mr. K. told us. ''And don't forget about utilities and insurance. Good luck to you all, and feel free to ask me for advice anytime.''

The bell rang and I gathered up my papers and books. I was going to try to catch up with Clay, but he was out the door before I could even get his attention. He certainly didn't seem brokenhearted about the way things had worked out.

Mr. Kirkpatrick smiled at me when I stopped beside his desk. His thick glasses were smudged and that silly bow tie he always wore was so crooked that I was tempted to reach out and straighten it for him. Sometimes he came to school so rumpled you'd think he slept in his clothes, but he was nice and I liked him most of the time. He never talked down to me the way a lot of my teachers did.

"Mr. Kirkpatrick," I said, deciding to plunge right in, "I think you must have made a mistake when you paired me up with Paul Ryan. I've never even met Paul and I'm sure we have nothing in common. I'd feel much more comfortable with this experiment if you'd let me have someone else as a partner."

"Someone like Clay?" he asked.

I felt myself blush right up to the roots of my hair. My feelings were always terribly obvious, even though I'd tried over and over not to be so transparent. If Mr. K. had noticed how I felt about Clay, then the whole school was probably talking about it.

"I just think it would make more sense for my partner at least to be someone I know," I said.

But Mr. K. was shaking his head, and he had that stubborn look on his face that he always got when a student attempted to sway one of his decisions.

"I chose Paul for you for a reason, Marcy," he said.

"To drive me crazy?"

He laughed, then removed his glasses and rubbed the little dent on his nose. "No, not to drive you crazy. You're one of my best students, Marcy, and so is Paul. I think you'll do well with this experiment."

"Are you sure about that? You won't change your mind?"

He shook his head.

I clutched my books tightly as I left the classroom. I should have known better than to even try. The next few months were going to be one long haul!

I was so busy fuming over the unfairness of it all that I didn't see Paul until I smacked right into him. My books flew in about five different directions, and my contact lenses nearly popped out of my eyes, I hit him so hard.

"I'm sorry," he said, speaking the first words I'd ever heard come out of his mouth. He stooped and began to pick up my books.

"*I'm* the one who walked into *you*," I pointed out, for some reason irritated by the way he was willing to take the blame. We were just outside the classroom door, and I wondered if he'd heard what I'd said to Mr. Kirkpatrick. I hoped not. Just because I didn't want him for a partner didn't mean I wanted to hurt his feelings.

Together we gathered up my scattered books and papers. When he handed me the last of them I looked at him to thank him. That was when I noticed for the first time that his eyes were light green, the same color as the ocean when the sun was at its highest. He smiled at me and I realized that he wasn't really stuck up, as I'd always assumed.

"Looks like we'll be working together," he said. "We'd probably better set up a time to get together and do some of the groundwork. I think the first couple of weeks will be the hardest, and then after that we should have the routine figured out."

If he'd heard me talking to Mr. K., he was giving no indication.

"We can get most of it done in study hall, can't we?" I asked.

"I doubt it. We have to find an apartment. And find out what utilities, insurance and furniture will cost."

I nearly dropped my books again. "You don't mean *really* look at apartments, do you? People will think we're nuts!"

"We won't rent anything, of course. But we should look at a few, to get a realistic idea of what we can afford to live in with our budget. We can explain that it's a class experiment and that we're just looking." He began to walk beside me as I headed for my locker. "It'll be a good experience for us. It'll give us a chance to find out what we're in for. It might even be fun."

Fun? I didn't see how that was possible, but I did see the logic in his suggestion. If we were going to take this whole thing seriously and work toward getting as good a grade as possible, we would have to do the research.

We were at my locker, and Paul was waiting for my decision. "Okay," I said. "It makes sense."

"How about if we meet tomorrow afternoon in the library," he suggested. "We can look through the newspaper ads there."

I agreed, and Paul left. I stood there staring after him for a moment. This project might prove more complicated than I'd originally thought. I wasn't at all convinced that I had the perfect partner.

Daphne appeared like magic at my side, her curly red hair bouncing and her face full of curiosity. "I saw you stop and talk to Mr. K. after class. Did you throw yourself on his mercy and beg him to change your partner? Did it work? Did you break the news to Paul?''

"I didn't beg, I merely asked. And, no, it didn't work.'' I opened my locker and shoved in the books I wouldn't be needing.

"That's too bad.''

"It sure is. But there's no point worrying about that now. Maybe Paul isn't as bad as we think. He's quiet, but is that a major crime? And he seems to be taking the experiment seriously. That's better than being stuck with someone who won't do his share of the work and will drag my grade down. Did you ever notice that his eyes are green?''

Daphne looked at me as though I'd suddenly grown an extra nose. "What's that got to do with economics?''

"Nothing,'' I said as I slammed my locker shut. "It's just that I've never seen eyes quite that color before.''

"Well, forget Paul's eyes,'' she said, "and concentrate on whether you're coming to the basketball game tonight.''

"Of course I am!'' I'd never missed a Friday night yet, and wasn't planning to now, especially as Clay had already said something about going out for a Coke afterward.

The thought brought me back to reality, and I began to plan what I would wear that evening to make Clay sit up and take notice.

Chapter Two

Clay had the ball and was racing across the court, dribbling for all he was worth. He leaped high into the air just as the guard from the other team made a desperate lunge for the ball. Clay and the other guy collided in midair, making a sound like the time my little sister stepped on a full box of Rice Krispies.

They fell to the floor and I jumped to my feet along with everyone else in the gym and strained to see over the heads blocking my view. That was one of the disadvantages of being short— half the time I couldn't see what was going on.

The gym was filled to capacity, and even though it was chilly outside, the body heat inside made the humidity level high. My perm was frizzing out of control and I felt too hot in the red-and-white sweater I'd worn. I envied the players down on the court, dressed only in their uniforms of shorts and sleeveless tops.

A foul was called against the other player, and I watched as Clay made the free throw, bringing the score to 46-42, with our side behind.

When the halftime buzzer sounded a large part of the crowd left their seats to get refreshments. I stayed where I was, waving to Daphne to come join me.

Daphne was a cheerleader mainly because she knew how good she looked in the short outfit. She wasn't really fired with school spirit and didn't really love cheering for our team, but she knew that her legs were definitely great and that her cheerleading outfit showed them off beautifully.

"Hi," she said, climbing up the bleachers and sitting at my side. She set her pom-poms down at her feet. "Great game, huh? Clay is at his best tonight, even if the other team is playing dirty. Well, just let them. Pretty soon all their starting players will foul out and they'll have to play their second string. Then we'll catch up and smash them!''

I looked at her in surprise. Usually Daphne sat through halftime complaining about her sore feet and the heat in the gym. When she was down there on the sidelines and cheering she did a good job of it, but very few people actually knew that she found the whole thing pretty silly. This was the first time I'd seen her take a genuine interest in a game.

''What's going on?'' I asked. ''Usually the only reason you want our team to win is so everyone will be in a good mood afterward. Why is this game different?''

She leaned close to me. ''Did you see that big guy who fouled Clay?''

''Number 14. How could I miss him?''

''Well, I dated him a couple of times last summer. He broke my heart and I hope we murder his team!''

I looked at Daphne, then burst out laughing. ''You've broken a few hearts in your day,'' I said, ''but I happen to know that no one has ever even dented yours.''

''Okay, maybe he didn't. But he did dump me and that hurts. You'll find out someday.''

I wondered if that was a not-so-gentle reminder from Daphne that she considered herself more mature simply because she was a year older than I. Either that, or she was commenting on the fact that Clay was my first boyfriend and she'd already had at least a dozen. Either way, I wasn't sure I liked what she was saying.

"What's that supposed to mean?" I asked, sitting up straight so that I seemed taller.

Daphne looked contrite. "Nothing. I'm sorry, really. The truth of the matter is that I'm insanely jealous because you have a date after the game and I don't."

"Why don't you go out with Hank?" I suggested. "You said he's been asking you for a long time."

"Puh-leez! Me and the captain of the chess team? What could we possibly have in common?"

"He's crazy about *you*. That's one thing you'd have in common."

Daphne picked up her pom-poms and got to her feet. "I'd rather let him worship me from afar," she said. "Tonight Dot and I are going to do something together and we'll probably spend the entire evening discussing the worthlessness of men. That is, unless we find a couple of guys to go out with."

"I've always admired your consistency, Daphne."

"Thanks. It's called being flexible. But enough of this chatter, I'd better get back down there, halftime is almost over. Keep your fingers crossed for our team." She bounded down the bleachers, curls flying and the back of her skirt flipping up. I might have known it wouldn't be school spirit that motivated her enthusiasm. Daphne had been boy conscious for as long as I could remember.

I looked around as some of the spectators began to return to their seats. I knew almost everyone, and waved to several people. Dot Van Atta stopped to gab for a minute and told me how much she liked my sweater. A couple of guys I recognized as seniors descended on us and began to flirt. Seeing her opportunity, Dot explained to them that I already had a date but that she and the pretty little red-haired cheerleader down below were going out for Cokes after the game and they were welcome to come along. The two seniors immediately lost interest in me, giving Dot all their attention.

I didn't see Paul anywhere, but that didn't surprise me, either. He'd never come to any of the school's sporting events, as far as I knew. What did he do with his time outside school. Just study? I found myself wondering what he did for fun.

Our team lost the game by a mere two points, much to Daphne's obvious distress. After the final buzzer had sounded I saw a player from the other team approach her, but she turned up her freckled nose and stalked off. I was glad she had a date after the game—even though she didn't know it yet. It would make her feel better.

"We would have won if Frankel hadn't fouled out in the third quarter."

"Nah, that didn't make any difference. Spence being out sick is what really hurt us. And Keaton's knee was bothering him again."

"Did you see how mad Coach was? He could have spit nails!"

"He'll have us running laps for a week."

"He can't blame us. That team is murder, we did pretty well keeping up the way we did. Two points. We really gave them a run for their money."

I sat squashed between Clay and another basketball player in a booth at McDonald's. We were with several of the players, and so far I'd hardly had a chance to talk. All they wanted to do was go over the game, criticizing and analyzing until I thought I'd go crazy. There was only one other girl with our group, the date of one of the other players. She looked bored by it all, too, but I couldn't even talk to her because I would have had to shout to be heard. I sipped my Coke through a straw and tried to look interested.

This wasn't what I'd had in mind when Clay suggested we do something after the game. I'd been looking forward to having a little time alone with him. Instead, I was with a bunch of jocks who didn't seem to know I was there.

I glanced at my watch and saw that it was getting late. Clay was in training and had to be in early, so I nudged him and pointed to my watch to remind him.

"We'd better get going," he said, sliding out of the booth and taking my hand. We left McDonald's and walked toward his car. "Guess we didn't have much time together tonight, did we?" he said.

"No, we didn't," I agreed. I was surprised that he'd noticed.

"I didn't plan it to be like this, but once we ran into the guys I couldn't help talking about the game. It would have been the same if we'd won. We would have spent all night talking about everything we did *right*." He smiled at me when we reached his car. Instead of getting his keys, he put his hands on my shoulders and looked up at the flawless night sky.

"I had fun," I lied.

"Well, next time it will be just the two of us," he said. "What would you like to do? See a movie? Go to the amusement park?" He snapped his fingers and looked pleased. "I know what we can do. There's an antique car show in the mall this weekend. We can go to that tomorrow."

I would have preferred a movie, but at least he was saying he wanted to see me again. Now that our plans were made Clay opened the car door and we got in. "Who did you get as your partner for Mr. K.'s experiment in economics?" I asked as he backed out of the parking space.

"No one," he said. "I'm a bachelor with a well-paying job."

"That sounds easy." I nearly sighed with relief. He hadn't gotten Chelsea.

"I'll bet it doesn't *stay* easy. Mr. K. will throw a surprise at me somewhere along the way, I'll bet."

"Like what?"

He shrugged. "Unemployment, maybe marriage." I flinched. "Or an accident that will leave me with huge hospital bills to pay. My brother Cliff says he did this same experiment two years ago, and that Mr. K. throws as many obstacles in your way as he can. No one gets off easy."

I wondered what was in store for me and Paul. I also wondered why Clay hadn't asked who *my* partner was.

He parked his car in front of my house and turned off the motor. Then he moved closer to me and I forgot all about everything but him. He hadn't kissed me on either of our previous dates, and I'd wondered why. But I had the feeling he was going to kiss me now, and I was glad I'd only had a Coke, instead of the onion rings I'd considered.

Clay's arm snaked across the back of the seat, then pulled me gently to him. When he kissed me it was so smooth, so effortless, that I knew he'd had lots of practice. His experience made up for my lack of it, which was probably a good thing. My nervousness didn't even show, and when he drew back I smiled as though I'd been doing it for years.

"I'll see you tomorrow," he said. "And will you have time this weekend to look over that report of mine?"

"I'll do it Sunday," I promised. I was a wiz in English Lit, and I had agreed to help Clay by looking over his report for errors. He was having a little trouble in that class.

He kissed me again on the tip of my nose, then reached across me to push open my door.

It wasn't until I was inside my own bedroom that I remembered I was supposed to meet Paul at the library Saturday afternoon.

Chapter Three

"Marcy, wake up."

My sister B.J. jumped on the edge of my bed, sending me about three inches in the air. "Why?" I mumbled, burying my face in my pillow and trying to ignore her.

"Mom's gone shopping and she left a note on the refrigerator that we're to unload the dishwasher and put a roast in the Crockpot for tonight."

I opened one eye. "It doesn't have to be done right this second."

B.J. certainly could be a pest sometimes. She'd been practicing for most of her fourteen years so she was bound to be pretty good at it. I knew darn well the only reason she was telling me this was because she absolutely hated to see me enjoy the luxury of sleeping in the morning after a date. She wasn't allowed to go out with boys yet, so she usually tried to do some little thing to spoil it for me when I did.

Like me, B.J. had long dark hair hanging nearly to the middle of her back, but hers was straight while mine was wavy from a perm. Her eyes were the same dark brown, fringed with thick lashes and tilting up just the tiniest bit. We both looked like Mom, which Dad always said was a blessing. B.J.'s chin was a little more pointed than mine, and she was going to be taller than me soon, but other than that the resemblance was pretty remarkable. Which meant that when we were out in public and she got obnoxious I couldn't even pretend she wasn't related to me.

Right now she was shaking my shoulder. "Just because you were out all night with Clay doesn't mean you're going to leave me with all the work," she said.

"I was in at eleven," I reminded her. "Now get lost and let me sleep."

She turned on the radio in our room and began yanking open drawers as she looked for something to wear. I pulled the blanket over my head and tried to ignore the racket. She was bound to get bored soon and leave me in peace.

But she only got worse. Soon she was stomping around, rattling closet doors and singing out of tune with the song on the radio.

I sat up straight in bed. "Barbara June!" I yelled. "I'm going to strangle you if you don't get out of here!"

No one *ever* called B.J. Barbara June. She stared at me in horror and ran from the room.

Of course I felt awful. Sleep was impossible, so I got out of bed and walked out to the kitchen in my nightshirt. I found B.J. there, unloading the dishwasher.

I took the roast out of the refrigerator and put it in the Crockpot. After sprinkling it with some salt and pepper I covered it with the lid.

"I'm going to look at apartments this weekend," I said casually.

"You're *what*?"

Briefly I explained the experiment to her.

"You mean you'll be shopping for groceries and furniture and everything?"

"We'll go to stores and make price lists," I said. "But we won't actually buy anything." I took the silverware from the dishwasher and put it away in the drawer. Companionably, we worked together for a few minutes straightening up the kitchen.

"What did you do on your date last night?" she asked. "Did you have fun?"

"Clay kissed me good-night."

"He did?" Her voice was an impressed whisper.

"I don't think it meant as much to him as it did to me, though," I admitted. "He's gone out with so many girls, he's probably kissed a hundred of them. I wish it could have been special for both of us."

"Is Clay the first boy who ever kissed you?"

I sat down at the kitchen table and propped my chin on one fist. "No, not the first. Remember last summer, when the people next door had their nephew from Texas visiting?"

"He kissed you?"

I smiled at the memory. "We went bike riding a few times, and the day before he left we went to the beach and watched the boats. He kissed me then. It was very nice, but a little sad because I knew he was leaving."

B.J. was enormously impressed. She had visions of me as Juliet and our neighbor's nephew as Romeo, torn apart by circumstances. I didn't spoil it for her by telling her he was just a very nice boy whom I'd only missed for about two days.

"How come Clay isn't doing the experiment with you?" she asked, bringing us both back to the present.

"Our partners were assigned to us by the teacher. We didn't get to make a choice. I'm going to the library after lunch to meet Paul and begin work. Do you want to come along?"

"Sure!"

B.J. and I finished the kitchen work. Then I called Clay to tell him I couldn't go to the antique car show with him after all.

"Will you still have time to look over that report?" he asked.

"Yes, I'll check it for you and give it to you Monday in school." I was disappointed that he didn't suggest we do something that night instead.

B.J. and I cleaned our room, had a quick lunch and got to the library shortly after one o'clock. As always on a Saturday afternoon, the library was full. We found Paul sitting at a table near the rear, already studying the rental ads in the local newspaper. We sat with him, and he showed me several possibilities he had noted.

"This one is furnished," he said, pointing at the paper with his pen. "Which will save us money on furniture. But the rent's a little higher. This one is reasonable, but it's an older building, which means it probably won't be well insulated so the heating bill might be high. I know you don't have to do much in the way of heating around here, but every little bit helps."

I pointed to an interesting-looking ad. "What about this one? It's near the mall, and that's where I work, according to Mr. K.'s instructions."

"The rent is outrageous."

"But we'll save money on gas because I'll be able to walk to work."

"But you only work part-time. I work full-time and this apartment is across town from my job, so we won't really be saving on gas."

"That's a new section of town," I pointed out. "So the buildings will probably be energy efficient. *And* it's near the business school where I'll be going to night classes."

B.J. was taking this all in, her eyes jumping from Paul to me and back to Paul again. "You guys sound really funny, you know that?" she said. "You might as well be really married!"

Paul smiled. "Well, we are in a way, according to the experiment, at least. This is to help

teach us to deal with real-life situations someday."

"Can I come along with you to look at
apartments?"

"Sure," he said, without even asking me. I
was glad he was being nice to my little sister, but
that didn't mean I wanted her hanging around
all day. B.J. was a little bit of a flirt, and there
was every possibility that she would end up em-
barrassing me. But she looked so happy when he
said that she could come along that I didn't have
the heart to say otherwise.

We wrote down a few of the most interesting
listings, then Paul went to the pay phone in the
library and made appointments to see the
apartments. He explained each time that it was
a class project and that we were only interested
in looking. One man told him not to come over,
that he wasn't interested in showing an apartment to a bunch of kids who weren't going to
rent, but most of the people Paul talked to were
very nice about it and willing to help us out.

B.J. and I had walked to the library, and we
all three climbed into Paul's rusty old Mus-
tang. Despite the car's appearance, as soon as
the motor turned over I knew it was in good
running condition. The car purred like a pam-
pered cat, which was a switch from Clay's late-

model Monte Carlo, which looked sharp but was always breaking down on him.

The first apartment we looked at was the one I'd talked Paul into seeing, the one near the mall. I fell in love with it immediately. It was spacious, with three big rooms and an oversize bathtub.

B.J. wandered over to the window. "I can see my school from here!" she exclaimed. "I could come over every day and visit." She was so into it, she seemed to have forgotten it was only a school project.

While B.J. and I were admiring the little terrace, Paul was talking to the building manager about the utilities.

"It's way out of our league," he said a minute later, coming up behind me as I inspected the closets.

"No, it's not," I said. "We'll just cut back a little in some other area."

"It's unfurnished. We'll never be able to afford to buy furniture for it."

"My parents have a bunch of old stuff in the garage, left over from when we remodeled the rec room. They'll let us have that."

"The utilities are high. And he says we'd have to come up with a two-hundred dollar deposit.

Forget it, Marcy, we'll just have to find something else.''

I was getting angry. What was the use of pretending if we couldn't pretend ourselves into a nice apartment? If money got tight I could pretend to inherit a fortune from a long-lost aunt. Actually, that was against the the rules, but why did Paul have to be so literal about everything? It was getting downright boring.

We looked at three more apartments before we found one that Paul thought we could afford. I looked around in horror at the dingy brown walls poorly lit by dirty light bulbs suspended from the ceiling. B.J. made caustic comments about the peeling paint and the cracked linoleum on the kitchen area.

"It's horrendous!" I whispered to Paul, keeping my voice low so that I wouldn't hurt the feelings of the man who was showing it to us.

"We could fix it up," Paul said cheerily in an audible voice. "It definitely has possibilities. You could whip up some curtains and dig up some old rugs—"

"I don't sew," I said firmly.

What kind of a person did he think I was anyway? The kind who wore little frilly aprons and baked brownies? I was getting tired of Paul's holy-moley attitude and I was also getting very tired of looking at apartments. We'd been at it all afternoon and we couldn't agree about any of them. Every time I thought we'd found the perfect one, Paul would say there was no way we afford it, and the ones that he found suitable were, in my opinion, substandard. My feet were beginning to hurt and B.J. was getting cranky. By the time he dropped us off in front of our house we were a silent and subdued threesome.

"I know you weren't crazy about that last one," he said, reaching over to open the car door for us, "but look at it this way. Mr. Kirkpatrick will be pretty impressed by our research, and you have to admit, learning to budget is what this course is all about."

I sighed. "I know you're right," I agreed grudgingly. "And I want to get a good grade just as much as you do, so I'll go along with that grungy apartment with the leaking faucets and sagging floors, but lighten up, can't you? There's no reason we can't have some fun, too—"

"I thought we were," he said, surprising me. Well, he'd certainly had me fooled, and judging by the way that B.J. was shuffling up our walk, it hadn't been her idea of a blast, either.

Chapter Four

Clay thumbed through his four-page report, his frown deepening as he saw all the notes I'd made in the margins.

We were in our second period study hall, sitting across from each other at the same table.

"How come it needs all these changes?" he asked. "I thought it was pretty good."

"The report itself isn't bad," I explained. "But you have a lot of mistakes in grammar and punctuation. And that lowers your grade."

"Oh. Well, that shouldn't be too hard to fix. But I don't know when I'll have time. I have basketball practice for an hour after school every day, and I have to study for an algebra test we're having at the end of the week." He pushed the papers toward me. "Could you help me out, Marcy?"

"Sure. We can spend the rest of this study hall going over it together." I knew that wasn't what he had in mind, but I was darned if I'd do all the work for him. I pretended not to notice his disappointment.

When the bell rang indicating the end of the second period, Clay and I walked down the hall together.

I still wasn't used to being seen with him. Several people stopped him to congratulate him on his performance Friday night, even though we'd lost the game. The girls who talked and flirted with him also smiled at me. These were the same girls who hadn't even known I existed. It was great for my ego.

It was even better with the guys. These were the same boys who had patronizingly called me kid, if they'd noticed me at all. Now that I was with Clay, they looked at me with different eyes, really noticing for the first time that I wasn't just some refugee from elementary school.

Clay and I parted when he had to go to algebra. I headed for the gym and my P.E. class.

Daphne caught up with me as I was changing into my shorts.

"I saw Chelsea watching you and Clay in the hall," she said. "I think she's jealous because you had a date with him Friday night."

"She has nothing to be jealous about," I said, reaching for my T-shirt, "I didn't have such a great time. Clay and his jock friends talked about the game all night, and the only time we were alone was when he drove me home. We've never talked about anything really. All he talks about is sports. I don't know anything about him and I don't get the feeling that he cares about me at all—as a person, I mean."

"Some guys just take longer to get to know," Daphne said.

I thought about Paul. Did I know much about him? I knew that he was quiet and serious. But I didn't know that much more. Why, for instance, didn't he come to any of the games? Why had no one ever been to his house?

"Hey," Daphne said, "you planning to spend the morning here? Those kids aren't going to wait for us, you know."

I tucked my shirt in my shorts and we jogged over to the volleyball court where a game had already started. Despite her lack of height, Daphne was a vicious spiker, and a popular player. When we finally got to play, our side won by a good margin.

By lunchtime we had worked up such an appetite that even cafeteria food sounded good. Daphne and I went through the line with enthusiasm. I took double helpings of nearly everything.

"I can come over tonight and help you let out the seams in all your clothes," Daphne said, eyeing my tray.

"I'm hungry. That volleyball game burned up a lot of calories."

She shook her head. "I don't know where you put it. Someone as little as you shouldn't be able to eat the way you do without blowing up like the Goodyear Blimp. It's not fair to the rest of us who have to watch every bite."

We found some space at a table and sat beside each other. Daphne was right, in a way. I was one of those lucky people who could eat pretty much what they wanted. Secretly, I harbored the fear that someday it might catch up with me and I would suddenly begin to gain weight. Maybe not, though, because my mother was still small and slender and she was nearly forty.

I dove enthusiastically into my food, oblivious of my surroundings until Daphne poked me hard in the ribs. "Look who's coming," she whispered.

Paul was approaching the table. When he stopped beside me, I slid over so that he could sit down.

"Hi," he said. "I called the utility companies during the study hall this morning and got an average figure on what our utilities will cost in that building." He shoved a piece of paper at me and I looked down at the numbers he'd written.

"Oh. Okay," I said. Why couldn't he wait until economics class to give me this information? This was our lunch break, and I usually tried to avoid spending it discussing school work. "Where's your lunch?" I asked.

"I ate already."

"Well, I didn't," I said, reaching for my food again. Daphne was strangely quiet.

"Do you have time to work a little more on this project after school today?" Paul asked.

"I suppose," I said. "What did you have in mind?"

"We'll need to figure out a budget, something that we won't have any trouble sticking to. Now that we have our apartment and utilities figured out, the budget is the last thing left to do."

"Okay."

He lowered his voice and spoke so that only I could hear. "Maybe when we're finished we can go have a pizza," he said. Grabbing his jacket and books, he got up to leave.

I looked after him in astonishment.

"What did Paul say to you?" Daphne asked with unabashed curiosity.

"I think he asked me for a date."

"Well, what did you say?"

"He didn't give me a chance to answer."

"We moved here from Montana last August," Paul said. He cut into the large pepperoni and mushroom pizza and handed me a piece.

"Just you and your parents?"

"Well, actually, just me and my mom. My dad died about three years ago."

"I'm sorry," I said. "It must be kind of hard, just the two of you." I thought about my own family. B.J. could be a pain in the neck, but I couldn't imagine not having her around, and I couldn't see dealing with Mom without having Dad to mediate.

"We get on fine," Paul said, as if in answer to my unspoken thoughts. "Although I worry about what will happen to her when I go to college. That's why I'm going to San Diego State. I couldn't go 'way off somewhere and leave her alone. I'm all she has now.''

"You can't take care of her forever, Paul. Sooner or later she's got to learn to live without you—"

"She's taken care of me for sixteen years," he said. "I don't intend to desert her now. And when and if the time comes for me to move, then I'll get her to move, too. She's a photographer, so she can take her work with her."

"I have twelve aunts and uncles and thirty-five cousins," I told him. I described my cousin Joy's wedding the month before and the crowd that had gathered at the reception afterward. "I hardly know most of my cousins, and there are a couple I've never even met."

"I'd like you to meet my mother sometime," he said. "I think you'd like her. But I'd better warn you, she'll probably want to take your picture."

"I'd like to meet her," I said.

Then I told Paul more about my family. He'd already met B.J., of course, so I told him my dad was a pharmacist and my mother the manager of Wexler's Speed Printing just a few blocks from the pizza parlor. I told him B.J. had a crush on him, but that he shouldn't take it too seriously because she was at that age where she fell in love with everyone from the mailman to her eighth-grade math teacher.

"You mean it isn't my charm and sophistication she fell for?"

"No, and it wasn't your gorgeous green eyes, either," I said. "You won her over when you let her go with us Saturday. She figured that was a sure sign that you were secretly in love with her and were just waiting for an opportunity to ditch me."

Paul laughed. "I like your sister," he said.

I leaned forward. "Paul," I said urgently, before I could stop myself. "Please shut me up if I sound nosy, but I want to ask you something. How come you don't participate in school activities? You don't give anyone a chance to know you. If we didn't have this project together, I probably wouldn't even be speaking to you—"

"I don't have the time," he said. "I have to work after school to earn money for college. I can't depend on the little my mother makes."

"How come you could get here today?"

He smiled mysteriously.

"Well?" I probed.

"We had to work on our project, didn't we?"

"Yes, I guess so."

It wasn't quite the answer I'd hoped for, but it would have to do for now. Besides, did he count our hour at Happy Joe's Pizza as "work on the project"? I was inclined to doubt it.

the project. I was incapable of doing

Chapter Five

Mom and Dad were sitting at the kitchen table by the time I got home. Mom was paying bills, her fingers expertly hitting the buttons of the calculator, the checkbook open in front of her. Dad was leaning over the want ad section of the newspaper, his glasses slipping down to the end of his nose. He was circling items with a pen.

"What are you looking for?" I asked, pulling up a chair. By reading upside down I saw that he was in the used-car section and my heart flipped over hopefully. Could it be they were finally starting to believe my claim that I needed wheels of my own?

Dad quickly dashed my hopes. "I'm thinking of trading in the station wagon for a van," he said. "That way we could use it to go camping and there'd be plenty of room for all of us."

"Oh." I tried hard not to look too disappointed, but besides the fact that I wouldn't be getting a car, I *hated* camping. B.J. and I both hated it, but Mom and Dad loved it. I figured this was because Mom had grown up in a small town just across the border in Arizona, and Dad had lived on a farm until he'd gone to college and met Mom. They liked that outdoorsy stuff. But B.J. and I had lived in La Mesa all our lives and we had never learned to enjoy a weekend of hungry insects and wild animals.

Mom pushed her calculator aside. "How'd your date go?"

"Fine," I answered. "We went out for pizza."

"You know you could have asked him in for a while. It's still early, and you know we like Clay."

"It wasn't Clay."

I knew this would be a bomb. I could tell by Mom's face what she was thinking. For years my only friends had been Daphne and a few other girlfriends, and now all of a sudden, I had not one, but two, boyfriends? There was no point explaining. And, in any case, I was sure that once she got over her amazement, she would be delighted to think that finally I was coming out of what she constantly referred to as my "shell."

"Who was it then?" she finally asked, when she'd somewhat recovered from the shock of my instant, surprising popularity.

"Paul Ryan. He's a new boy at school. He and his mother moved here from Montana," I babbled before she could ask me about his entire life history. I'd never thought about it before, but that must have been why all his clothes had been so heavy. He'd probably not yet had either the time or the money to buy more appropriate ones.

My mom was smiling brightly, even expectantly.

"I met him working on an economics project. Mr. Kirkpatrick assigned him to me as a partner."

My mom visibly relaxed. "I think I heard B.J. talk about him," she said.

"It fits," I said, "and now if you guys will excuse me, I think I'll hit the old sack. I've got kind of a busy day tomorrow...."

Unfortunately, the family third degree wasn't over yet. When I got to the bedroom, B.J. sat up straight in her bed, and started to fire off her questions.

"Did you have fun? Do you like him? Did he kiss you? I tried watching from the window, but I couldn't see that much."

"Come on, B.J. What is this? An army inspection? Besides, I've told you many times not to spy on me."

"How am I going to learn anything if I can't watch you?" she asked. "You're my role model. I have to know what I'm going to be in for in a couple of years. *Did* he kiss you?"

I threw my T-shirt and jeans in the hamper in the closet and pulled a nightshirt over my head. "No, he didn't," I admitted. "I thought he was going to, but then at the last minute he seemed to change his mind."

"So why didn't you kiss *him*? I would have."

"I don't know. I thought about it." I pulled the covers back from my bed and sat down on the edge of the mattress. B.J. had a couple of her stuffed animals on her bed and I picked them up and threw them at her. She was at the age where a part of her had outgrown her stuffed toys, but another part of her still hated to part with them.

Right now I thought I could understand how she felt. I also felt torn in two different directions. For the past three years, ever since I'd started high school, I'd thought Clay Buckland was the most special person in the state of California. I'd never for one minute believed he'd even notice me, so when he'd asked me out it was like I'd suddenly won every sweepstakes I'd ever entered. It was simply too good to be true.

So why did I keep thinking about Paul? And why had I been so disappointed when he hadn't kissed me?

"I can't believe you passed up an opportunity like that," B.J. said. She rolled over on her side so that her back was to me. In a few minutes I could hear her gently snoring.

The weather turned warm again and a bunch of us decided it was beach time. The water was way too cold to swim in—although there were always a few brave souls who didn't mind turning blue—but it was perfect bonfire weather.

On Saturday night, we packed enough food to feed a baseball team for a year and headed for Mission Beach.

Daphne had decided, after being forced to work with Hank on the economics project, that he wasn't so bad after all, and she had invited

him along. Together they started building a
bonfire on the sand while Clay and I unpacked
the trunk of his car. He'd gotten a B on his report, plus we'd won the game against one of our
toughest competitors the night before, so he was
in a terrific mood.

"I really needed that grade," he said as he
pulled several wire clothes hangers from a sack
and handed them to me. "Mrs. Del Marco told
me that she'd always known I had it in me, and
that she expected me to keep up the good
work."

He seemed to have forgotten that he'd had a
little help with the report, but I didn't remind
him. I didn't want to spoil it for him.

We carried as much as we could to the flick-
ering bonfire, and saw that several people had
already arrived. Dot was there with her new
boyfriend, and so were Bucky Spence, Drew
Hoffman and several other members of the
varsity basketball team, all with dates.

We spread blankets around the growing fire
and Clay took the wire clothes hangers and un-
bent them until they were as straight as he could
get them. Then we stuck jumbo-size marshmallows on the ends of them and held them out to
the fire.

I sat close to Clay on our blanket, watching as my marshmallow turned a light golden brown.

"It's done," Clay said.

"I like mine cooked really dark," I told him. "Almost black on the outside. Then it's extra soft and squishy on the inside."

"Yuk," he said, and popped his own golden marshmallow into his mouth.

On the other side of the fire I could see that Daphne and Hank were roasting hot dogs on the end of their wires.

"Clay," I began, "what's your family like?"

"They're like any other family," he said.

"No two families are the same. You told me you have a brother named Cliff. Do you have any other brothers or sisters?"

"I have a sister named Diana who is married and lives in Sacramento. Hand me the marshmallows, will you?"

I handed him the package. "What do your parents do?"

He impaled a new marshmallow with his wire. "Why the big interest? You're here with me, not them."

"Well, what do you want to do after high school? Are you going to college?"

"Most likely. My parents expect me to." He leaned forward and concentrated on getting his marshmallow evenly cooked.

Trying to get information out of Clay was like trying to pull teeth from a tiger. I finally gave up. He really only liked talking about school or our friends, I decided. Soon he and the other boys began to rehash the game from the night before. He didn't even try to include me in the conversation.

I got up and went to sit beside Daphne. Hank had gone to his car for another six-pack of soda pop.

"Doesn't the fire feel good?" she asked, holding her hands out to the warmth. "Hey, what's wrong?"

"I don't know." I sighed. "Daphne, tell me the truth. What do you think of Clay?"

"He's gorgeous. He's popular. He's the captain of the basketball team, which is a real honor considering he's only a junior. Need I say more?"

"Why did he and Chelsea break up?" I asked. It shouldn't have mattered to me. The past was the past, but I wanted to know. "They seemed like the perfect couple."

"I'm really not sure," she told me. "Although I have heard that it was Clay's doing. He seems to be the kind of guy who likes to play the field. I do know he's dated a lot of girls. There's nothing wrong with that, I guess, as long as he's honest with you about it. Do you think he's going out with other girls?''

''I haven't really thought about it.'' I pulled my feet in and rested my chin on my knees.

I opened a can of pop and looked around. Other than Daphne and sometimes Dot, this wasn't a crowd I'd hung around with much in the past. The hockey captain's date was the junior class homecoming attendant. The class president was sitting on the other side of the fire with his arm around the shoulders of a girl with long blond hair. These were the most popular kids in school. A month ago I'd been on the outside looking in. Now I was part of the group. I was honest enough with myself to admit that it was because of Clay. He had brought me into this magic circle. Wasn't that what I'd always wanted?

I went back to where Clay was sitting and carefully toasted my marshmallow a nice crinkly black. Just the way I'd always liked them.

Chapter Six

My parents traded in our comfortable old station wagon for a shiny new van and began making plans for a camping weekend. B.J. developed a rash on her arms that she claimed came from merely *thinking* about poison ivy. I kept my fingers crossed that their plans would never materialize, even though I knew it was hopeless. I'd have to face at least one weekend squeezed into a sleeping bag the size of a shoebox. I'd end up so stiff that I'd walk funny for a week afterward, but Mom and Dad would love every minute of it.

I saw less of Paul now that the groundwork on our project had been completed. There wasn't much left to do, except for a little book-keeping. We talked a few times during class, about the experiment mostly, but since things were going so smoothly there wasn't much to say.

Mr. Kirkpatrick complimented me one day after class about the careful research we'd done. He seemed to assume that I was the one who'd insisted on perfection. I had to set him straight.

"Paul was the one who wanted to look at real apartments," I admitted. "It was kind of fun. I was surprised at how much they cost."

He looked at me through glasses so smudged I wondered how he could see. "Expenses always run higher than you expect. How are you doing with the rest of it? Any problems?"

"No. Paul really pays attention to details. We picked an apartment, haunted some second-hand shops for inexpensive furniture and he even figured up our mileage for getting to our jobs and to my classes. He didn't leave out a thing."

"Then you're not still sorry I matched you up with him?"

"It's probably the best thing you could have done for me. We're sure to get a terrific grade." Hint, hint.

As it turned out, my optimism was a little premature. Just when I thought we'd gotten over the hardest part, Mr. Kirkpatrick threw a monkey wrench into the machinery.

"I've been laid off," Paul told me, his face long and his hands buried deep in his pockets.

It was just after lunchtime and I was standing at my locker. I slammed the door shut. "How could you get laid off? I thought most of your jobs were helping your neighbors—they can't all have fired you—"

"Of course not. I mean I've been laid off from the job Mr. Kirkpatrick gave me."

"*What?* When? Why?"

I had to wait until after school to find out. The suspense was unbearable. I kept looking at the clock on the wall, trying to make it go faster through sheer willpower. I looked at the clock so many times that Mr. Dern asked in front of the whole class if I had a hot date.

At three-thirty I found Paul waiting for me by the front of the building. He looked depressed.

"What happened?" I asked.

"I just found out today, in economics class. Mr. Kirkpatrick gave me a piece of paper saying I'd been laid off from my job and would be eligible for unemployment benefits. But the money from unemployment isn't nearly enough to get us by. I tried to tell you right after class, but you took off too fast." He sat down on the step and I sat beside him. All around us kids were hurrying to leave, anxious to get to their jobs, or the beach or home. We sat for a while in gloomy silence.

"That's not fair," I said finally. "We were doing so well, why did he have to do this to *us*?"

"He wasn't picking on us," Paul told me. "It's just the way he runs this experiment. I heard that a couple of the other kids also lost their jobs, and that Clay Buckland not only is a recent groom, he had a fire in his apartment and lost everything. I hope he had renters' insurance."

"He didn't," I said. Clay had proudly shown me his budget at the beginning of the experiment, but when I'd pointed out to him that he'd neglected to take out insurance he'd been unconcerned. Now he was paying the price.

Paul balanced his schoolbooks on his knees. "Dot Van Atta had an accident and will be in the hospital for at least a month," he said.

I looked at him in shock, then realized he was still talking about the economics experiment.

"Oh, you scared me," I said, putting a hand on his arm. "This darned experiment. It's getting too true to life."

"That's the whole point."

"But why do disasters have to happen to all of us? Why can't someone win a lottery, or get a big raise?"

"There have been a few who got good news," he assured me.

"Just not us," I said bitterly. "What are we going to do? The rent is due in less than a week. Is this what my parents have been going through for the past twenty years? No wonder my dad has gray hair."

Paul was smiling, and suddenly he stood up. "This experiment is supposed to be like real life, right?"

"Right."

"Well, what would we do if we really were married and I'd just lost my job?"

I got to my feet and smiled. I was getting his drift. "We'd find jobs."

"Right." He nodded and put his arm around my shoulder. "So I'm going to go out and find another job. I've been planning to, anyway. The odd jobs I do around the neighborhood help out, but I'm going to need a real job if I want to go to college. I'll find a job, and then I'll go to

Mr. Kirkpatrick and tell him. I won't have to go on unemployment.''

I was so unstrung by the feel of Paul's arm around me that I hardly heard his words.

"What do you think?" he asked.

Of what? I wondered. Was he asking me if I liked having his arm around me? If he was, the answer was yes. Or was he asking me about the experiment?

"Well?" he asked. "Do you think Mr. K. will let me get away with it?"

"I'm not sure," I said. "He might not allow it."

"Why not? This whole thing is supposed to be to teach us about the real world. I'm not going to sit back and let him pull all the strings. If he told us we'd lost our apartment for some reason, we'd find another. Well, I'm going to find another job."

"But the experiment is just pretend," I reminded him. "So why can't you just pretend to find another job?"

"Because I have to prove to him that I really could do it," Paul said.

I saw the logic in this, and had to admire him for his determination. He still had his arm around me, and although the crowd had thinned out considerably I still saw a few kids looking at us curiously. Everyone knew I was dating Clay. I wondered how long it would take for this to get back to him, and if he would care.

"I think it's a terrific idea," I told Paul.

"Good. Can I give you a ride home?"

"Sure."

Along the way I saw one of those portable hot dog stands on the sidewalk. "Oh, look," I said, pointing. "Let's stop there. I love hot dogs."

"So do I," he said. "With mustard and relish."

"I like mine with chili and onion," I confessed. "But then I don't dare go near anyone afterward."

We left our books on the front seat of his car, then went to the hot dog stand. We each ordered, including two Cokes, then carried our food to a wooden bench under a big old shade tree.

"What are you going to study in college?" I asked after half of my hot dog was gone.

"I'm not sure. I know I'm supposed to have a clear idea of what I want to do with my future, but I just don't. I figure I'll take the basic business courses the first year, then when I decide for sure what I want to do I can always change my major. Some days I lean toward education, then other days I think I'll go into prelaw."

"Prelaw. Whew." I shook my head. "You're talking about a lot of years in school."

"I know. That scares me sometimes, too. That's when I start thinking that education would be the way to go. I've had so many terrific teachers over the years, I'd like to think that I could be like that. How about you? What do you want to study in college?"

"I used to want to be a model," I said, laughing. A little breeze had come up and my hair blew in my eyes. I pushed it back. "I'd practice looking glamorous in front of the mirror in my bedroom, and B.J. used to copy me. I'd pin my hair up on top of my head and wear enough mascara to glue my eyes shut, but I thought the modeling agents were going to be breaking my door down any day. The problem was, though, that I was just too shy to ever do anything about it. I was great at parading around in my own bedroom, but as soon as I got around people I froze. Eventually I realized I'd be better off using my brain than my looks. Besides, I'm way too short to be a model."

"I think you would have made a good model," Paul said. "You're certainly pretty enough. But I'm glad you changed your mind."

"Why?" I asked, pleased by the compliment.

"Because if you still wanted to be a model you'd be planning to take off to someplace glamorous like New York or Paris after school, then I'd never see you. At least this way I can hope you'll stay around."

He leaned toward me at the exact same moment that I leaned toward him. Our kiss would have been perfect if I hadn't been holding my hot dog in my hands between us. The chili dripping on my blue jeans sort of took the romance out of the moment. Besides, I needed a napkin.

Paul got one for me and we finished our hot dogs. He drove me home and I think he would have kissed me again in spite of the chili on my jeans, except that B.J. was sitting in the front yard playing with Butter, the yellow kitten she'd recently adopted.

I got out of his car, then leaned back in the open window. "When are you going to start job hunting?" I asked.

"Right away. I'm going to go home and change clothes, then I think I'll go and fill out applications at every business I can find open."

"Will you call me and let me know how it went?" I asked.

"You bet. Keep your fingers crossed for me."

I held up my right hand and showed him that I had two fingers crossed.

"Mom called and said she's going to be a little late getting home," B.J. told me after Paul had driven away. "She wants us to start supper."

"Okay." I bent over and scratched Butter's ears, then laughed as the kitten batted her little paw at my hand.

"Do you know *why* Mom's going to be late?" B.J. asked me.

"How could I know? You're the one who talked to her."

"She's going shopping for new sleeping bags."

"Oh, no," I groaned. Together we walked into the house, B.J. carrying the kitten in her arms. "They're really serious about this, aren't they?"

"Unfortunately, yes," B.J. said. She put Butter down on the floor as I went to the freezer and pulled out a pound of hamburger. I stuck it in the microwave to thaw while B.J. washed her hands and began peeling potatoes.

By the time Dad got home a short while later we had a hamburger pie well under way. He started chopping vegetables for a salad, so I had a little free time to call Daphne.

"I'm glad you called," she said breathlessly. "My demented brother has decided to clean out the garage and he wanted me to help. Have you ever seen the inside of a garage that hasn't had its door opened in almost two years? There must have been a million spiders in there, and who knows what else. But he bought this rusted out old jalopy and he thinks he needs the garage now. I tried to tell him that a little rain would only help the appearance of that car, but he wouldn't listen to me."

I tried to tell Daphne about Paul kissing me, but she seemed too intent on her own problems.

"What really makes me mad," she continued breathlessly, "is that last year when I'd saved up all my money from my summer job and wanted to buy a car my father wouldn't let me. He quoted all kinds of statistics about accidents involving teenage drivers. He told me so many horror stories that I was afraid to leave the house for a week. But now Brad, who's only had his driver's license for a month, is allowed to buy a car. This is discrimination, for sure."

"Daphne," I cut in, "Paul gave me a ride home from school today."

"See? Everyone has a car but me," she said.

"I don't have one," I reminded her. "But what I wanted to tell you was that Paul gave me a ride home, and we stopped off for hot dogs and he kissed me. And I kissed him back. Until the chili spilled on my lap, that is."

"I thought you said you had a hot dog."

"I had a chilidog."

"You kissed him after eating a chilidog? Weren't you worried about your breath?"

I got up from my bed, where I'd been sprawled, and closed the bedroom door. I didn't want anyone overhearing this conversation. "Daphne," I said, "didn't you hear me? I kissed Paul. Paul. I'm supposed to be going with Clay!"

"Has Clay ever said anything about going steady?" she asked.

"No."

"Then what's the problem?" she asked. "As far as I'm concerned, you have a great thing going. You like Paul and have to be with him sometimes anyway because he's your partner in economics, and Clay is pretty terrific, too. So what's wrong with seeing both of them?"

"It doesn't seem very honest," I said.

B.J. was rattling the bedroom door, demanding to be let in. I ignored her.

"You worry too much," Daphne said. "You're just like my dad. He worries all the time, too. If he trusts me to drive his car once in a while I don't see why he won't let me have my own car. I've had my license for well over a year and I haven't had so much as a fender bender."

I listened to Daphne for a few more minutes, then I made up some excuse to hang up and unlocked the door so B.J. could get in. She was fuming, but I hardly noticed.

Daphne and I had been best friends since junior high. We'd always accepted each other for what we were. She'd never minded that I was younger than everyone else in our class, and I was accustomed to the way she flitted from boy to boy. I figured she was just getting it out of her system, and that she'd get around to settling down one of these days.

We'd always been good for each other. Daphne introduced me to people, and I often thought that without her I'd have been too shy to make any friends on my own. Of course I wasn't nearly as shy as I used to be. I'd grown up a bit and I knew now that it wasn't as difficult as I'd always thought to just talk to people.

And I, in return, helped tone down Daphne's flamboyance. My practical nature had kept her from getting into quite a few jams. I'd spent a lot of time talking her out of doing things. She had a real flair for practical jokes, usually on teachers.

That's why I was so disturbed at the way she had hardly even listened to me on the phone. Right when I'd needed a sympathetic ear, she had practically ignored me. It left me feeling sort of sad. Who could I talk to if I didn't have Daphne?

"This is my room, too, you know." B.J. was still storming around, furious at having been locked out. "I've never locked you out, not even when I had my friends over."

B.J. mentioning her friends made me think of Daphne again, and my stomach got that hollow feeling that always happened when I was getting close to tears. I opened a magazine and tried to take my mind off what was going on in my life.

"Hey, what's wrong?" B.J. asked, peering into my face.

"Nothing. Leave me alone." I pushed her away and turned the pages of my magazine.

"You look awful. Was that Clay on the phone? Did he dump you?"

"No, he didn't dump me," I said irritably. "As a matter of fact, we have a date this weekend to go to the Hall and Oates concert."

"Mom and Dad are letting you go to a rock concert?" she asked in disbelief.

"Sure they are." Actually, I'd had to practically beg to get them to let me go to the concert with Clay, but I wasn't going to tell B.J. that.

B.J. sat on my bed, even though she knew that it was strictly off limits. "Then why do you look so sad?" she asked.

I shot her a dirty look. "B.J., it's personal, okay?"

"Maybe I can help."

"Don't be silly," I snapped.

B.J. looked so hurt that I felt guilty, though she could be a real pest at times. On more than one occasion I'd come into our room to find her trying on my clothes, once a brand-new pair of shoes that I hadn't even worn yet. She experimented with my makeup, and sometimes she talked in her sleep so much that she kept me awake half the night.

But I knew she wasn't as bad as some kid sisters. Several times she'd taken over baby-sitting jobs for me when something else had come up that I'd wanted to do, and once she promised to keep a secret you could pull her fingernails out one by one and she'd never tell.

But she was still just a kid sister, and not someone I could really talk to—especially about boys.

"You wouldn't understand," I said in a gentler tone of voice.

"How do you know, if you won't even give me a chance?"

"Good point," I said. What the heck, I decided. I needed to talk to someone, and if B.J. was the only person available then she'd just have to do.

I told her everything. How Clay was exciting to be with because his crowd were the class leaders, and how even though he sometimes ignored me to talk sports with his friends, when he did pay attention to me he could be very sweet and considerate. Once he'd left a funny little card in my locker, and I still had it, pressed between the pages of my yearbook.

Then I told her about Paul, and how comfortable I felt with him. He never ignored me. In fact, when I was with Paul he had a way of making me feel like I was the most important person in the world. He'd told me about his family, and had even invited me to meet his mother. I felt that I could ask Paul anything about himself and he would give me an honest answer.

"Do you see what I mean?" I asked when I was finished.

B.J. nodded. "I sure do. There's only one thing to do. Nothing."

I threw my hands up in the air. "Oh, great, B.J. That's terrific advice you're giving me here."

"No, listen to me. This is obviously something you can't make a hasty decision about. So the sensible thing is to see them both for a while, until you feel sure about one or the other. As long as neither has said anything about going steady, you're not doing anything underhanded."

You know, that kid made sense once in a while.

"Thanks, B.J.," I said.

Chapter Seven

I'd never been to a rock concert before and I wanted to wear the perfect outfit, have the perfect hairstyle and have an absolutely perfect evening. I knew how much the tickets had cost Clay, so I knew the night must be pretty special to him, too. I didn't want anything to go wrong to spoil it.

The concert hall was packed with kids. Clay and I fought our way to our seats, which turned out to be in about the sixth row from the front, right beside a gigantic speaker. When the music started I was tempted to stick my fingers in my ears to protect them from permanent damage. And besides the blaring music, there was the sound of several hundred fans screaming and clapping for all they were worth.

Hall and Oates were favorites of mine. I'd dreamed of seeing them in person for years, ever since I'd first started collecting their albums.

Now I realized that I would have been better off listening to their albums or watching them on the tube. Not only did the noise of the audience drown out their music, but these same fans refused to stay in their seats. I was being bumped and shoved around so much that I longed for the concert to end.

"They're great, aren't they?" Clay shouted in my ear.

"How can you tell?" I shouted back. I was getting a crick in my neck from trying to see past the people standing up in front of me, and my feet were killing me, they had been stepped on so many times.

"Whaaat?" Clay yelled, cupping his hand behind his ear.

"Never mind!" I just didn't have the nerve to tell Clay I was dying to leave. Not only had he paid all that money for the tickets, but he was having a ball. He didn't even seem to notice the deafening noise, the stampeding crowd. I gritted my teeth and looked forward to the end.

But relief was nowhere in sight. Not only did the concert seem to go on forever, but even after it was over it took us more than an hour to work our way through the crowd, out of the hall and into Clay's car.

"Wow! That was really something!" Clay exclaimed enthusiastically as he backed slowly out of the parking space.

"Definitely." I agreed, though in my heart of hearts I suspected that my definition of "really something" differed from Clay's. Why had I been so concerned about my appearance? If Clay had even noticed it, he hadn't bothered to mention it. I just wanted to go home and forget about the whole ghastly evening.

Then Clay surprised me. "We still have a little time," he said. "How about a walk on the beach?"

"Sounds good to me."

Clay turned off toward Pacific Beach, the beach closest to the concert hall. He parked the car and opened the door for me, then he took my hand and guided me toward the little path that led to the water.

When we got to the beach, we took off our shoes and rolled up our jeans. The sand felt wet

and squishy and I wiggled my toes with plea-
sure.

Clay put his arm around me. "I like the beach
at night," he said. "It's peaceful. Look at the
way the moonlight reflects off the waves. You
could almost believe in mermaids on a night like
this."

I looked up at Clay in astonishment. That was
just about the longest speech I'd heard him
make on a subject unrelated to sports. I'd never
suspected that he possessed such a romantic
streak. His words were almost poetic.

"We should come out here and dig for clams
some night," he suggested. "There are plenty of
them around."

"How can you tell?" I asked.

He pointed down to the wet sand at our feet.
"See there? That's a clam. All you do is watch
for the little bubbles in the sand, then dig like
crazy before he has a chance to burrow any
deeper."

"Do you come here often at night?" I asked.

"Not as often as I'd like. There's basketball
practice in the winter, softball and track in the
summer and football in the fall. It's probably
for the best, though. If I were free to come here
as often as I'd like I'd probably turn into a
beach bum."

We'd been walking for several minutes and hadn't met one other person. I was beginning to feel very romantic. I pretended that Clay and I were alone on a deserted island. No school to worry about, no reports to finish or deadlines to meet.

"It's about time to go back," Clay said.

I sighed as my fantasy island slowly sank into the sea.

We drove home in silence. I was thinking about how nice it would be if Clay and I could just be alone together more often. I liked him so much better when he wasn't trying to impress his basketball buddies.

"Do you want to come in for a few minutes?" I asked.

"Better not. I'll barely make curfew as it is. By the way, how are you coming along with typing my report?"

He'd given me ten pages of his nearly illegible handwriting to type over the weekend. As he had no typewriter, this had at the time appeared to be perfectly logical.

"I did it yesterday afternoon. I'll give it to you in school Monday," I said.

"Why don't you give it to me now?" he suggested. "I need it for my first class."

"Okay," I agreed. "Wait a sec. I'll just dash upstairs and get it."

Clay remained under the front porch light while I slipped into the house and crept into the bedroom to find the report that I'd left on my desk. When I came back outside with it, Clay stretched out an eager hand.

"Gee, thanks," he said. "You're the greatest." He leaned down and quickly brushed his lips over mine.

He had sprinted off toward his car before the ugly little thoughts began to form: if I'd refused to give him the report until Monday, would he still have called me the greatest, and more disturbing yet, would he even have bothered to kiss me at all?

Chapter Eight

"Marcy, did I wake you? I'm sorry." It was Paul on the phone.

"That's okay. It was about time for me to get up anyway. What's up?"

"I found a job."

I sat up in bed, wide awake. "When?"

"Yesterday afternoon. I tried to call you last night, but your father said you were out."

"Uh—yes. Where's your job?"

"In the stock department at Jessup's," he said.

"That's the big store in the mall. We shop there all the time. When do you start?"

"I start tomorrow. I'll work for a few hours every day after school, then a few hours on the weekends. I was lucky to get the job. They had a whole stack of applications."

"I wish I could get a job," I told him. "I had a summer job last year, at the Dairy Delight. But my father is dead set against my working during the school year. He's afraid my grades will suffer if I have a job."

B.J., who'd been puttering around the bedroom pretending not to listen, spoke up. "Your grades are going to suffer if you keep doing Clay's work for him."

I threw a pillow at her but she ducked out of the way.

"Are you busy today?" Paul asked. "Since this is probably the last weekend I'll have free for a while I thought it would be nice to do something."

I got out of bed and carried the phone with me to the closet. "What did you have in mind?"

"Do you have a bicycle?" he asked.

"Sure. Up until about a year ago it was my main source of transportation."

"I thought we could ride into San Diego. Go to the beach, or maybe the zoo. I haven't seen the zoo yet, but I've heard a lot about it."

A bike ride sounded like fun, but he was a little too ambitious for me. He was talking about straining muscles that I hadn't used in quite a while. San Diego, although only a few minutes away by car, suddenly seemed on the other side of the world.

"Marcy, are you still there?" Paul asked.

"I'm here," I said. "Are you sure you know what you're getting into? There are a lot of hills around that area."

"Do you good," he insisted, and I could hear the smile in his voice.

I melted. Besides, as a native of the area, wasn't it my moral obligation to show Paul, the newcomer, around?

"Okay." I laughed. "But give me a couple of hours to do some things around here. I think my father mentioned something about cleaning closets, and I know he expects me to help out."

"Two hours," Paul said. "Then I'll be at your doorstep with my trusty ten-speed. I'll supply the lunch. I make great cheese and avocado sandwiches."

"Yuck."

"Don't say that until you've tried one. See you shortly."

I hung up the phone and dressed quickly. I wanted to surprise Dad by offering to clean out the closets. I figured the sooner we got started the sooner we'd be finished.

He knew immediately that something must be going on for me to volunteer for one of my least favorite jobs, so after we'd finished the worst two he decided to call it quits.

"I might do the rest later," he said. "Or I might just leave them for next weekend. It's too nice a day to spend inside. Go ahead and do what you want now."

"Thanks, Dad." I cleaned up quickly and dressed in jeans and a bright red blouse that I tied in a knot in front. I packed a lightweight sweater in my backpack just in case it grew cool, then went to the garage to get my bike out of storage.

It had been in there ever since I'd gotten my driver's license, and was covered with a layer of dust and a few cobwebs. Taking an old rag from a hook on the wall, I began to clean it off.

"You haven't ridden that thing in a while, have you?"

I looked up and saw Paul standing in the open doorway.

"There's something about getting a driver's license that spoils a person," I said. "But I'm glad you suggested this. The more I think about it the more fun it sounds. I haven't been to the zoo in a couple of years myself." I gave the bike a last couple of swipes for good measure, and we were ready to go.

"Oh boy, am I rusty!" I exclaimed as I painfully began to pump up the hill by our house. I could feel the muscles in my calves straining in protest. By the next day I'd probably be stiff as a board.

Paul led the way as we merged with the traffic. After a while I forgot my aches and pains and began to enjoy myself. Soon I was easily keeping up with Paul, who was setting a fairly moderate pace.

It didn't take us too long to reach San Diego.

"How did you know the way?" I asked as I caught up with him.

"I looked at a map last night."

So he'd been planning this trip while I had been out with Clay! And all the time, I'd been hoping that Clay would pay more attention to me! In fact, I'd even had a whole desert island fantasy about Clay when we'd been walking on the beach. And yet here I was having a great time with Paul. I hadn't given Clay a single thought until that instant.

We were approaching Balboa Park. The area had become even more hilly and I began to feel tired. Paul looked across at me and slowed down.

"Tired?" he asked. "Want to stop for lunch?"

"I wouldn't mind resting for a while," I answered.

We turned off the street onto a bike path that took us into the prettiest part of the park. Even now, during the winter months, the park was alive with activity. We threaded our way through bikers and skaters.

A small black-and-white dog broke loose from its owner and began yapping at Paul's front wheel.

"Hey!" he shouted, "get out of here, you little mutt!"

I saw his bike wobble, then career off the path as he lost control and headed for a clump of spiky-looking bushes.

I jumped off my bike just as Paul, swerving to avoid the bushes, fell to the grass. A woman about my mother's age rushed up to grab the dog by the collar.

Paul landed on his shoulder and rolled, just like the stunt men in the movies. He sat up just as I reached him, looking dazed but unhurt.

"Is he all right?" the woman holding the dog asked.

He stood and stretched his legs experimentally. "Sure, I'm okay." He picked up his bike and examined it. "My bike's okay, too."

"Thank goodness," the woman said. She was holding the dog in her arms. "I'm terribly sorry. Misty's never attacked anyone before. The bike must have frightened her. Are you sure you're not hurt?"

"I'm fine," Paul assured her. She put down the dog and they walked away.

Paul took his bike by the handlebars and we headed for a nearby bench. "I guess this is as good a place as any to eat our lunch. The zoo is pretty near here, isn't it?"

"Not far." We propped our bikes up and sat on the bench.

Paul took off his backpack and looked inside. He didn't say anything, he just continued to stare inside the backpack.

"What's wrong?" I asked.

"Do you have any idea what smashed cheese and avocado sandwiches look like?" He closed the backpack and looked at me. "Believe me, it's not a pretty sight."

"Well, we can get something at the zoo," I said.

We were close enough to the zoo now that we could walk our bikes along the path. Paul limped slightly, but when I asked him about it he insisted it was nothing.

"There it is." I pointed straight ahead to the entrance to the zoo. "Look at the crowd. Everyone in the city must have had the same idea to come here today."

We paid our admission price, had the backs of our hands stamped so we could leave and come back later if we wanted, then entered the zoo.

"Let's see the monkeys first," I said, grabbing Paul's arm. "I'd forgotten how much fun this place is. Wait until you see the seals. You can buy little containers of fish if you want to feed them. A lot of animals aren't even in cages."

"Not in cages? What do they do, roam around loose?"

"They're kept in their area by wide, deep trenches that they can't get across," I explained. "Even the lions and the bears. It used to scare me when I was little, but in all these years I've never heard of any animal jumping across one of those trenches.''

We bought a couple of cheeseburgers from a nearby snack stand, then went to watch the monkeys.

"Look at that one there," Paul said, pointing. "Doesn't he remind you of Coach Boggs?"

"Yes." I giggled. "He's even bowlegged like Coach Boggs. All he's missing is the whistle hanging around his neck."

"Any minute I expect him to make all the other little monkeys start running laps around the cage," Paul said.

We threw our empty wrappers in the nearest trash bin and walked on. We looked at the sleek, shiny seals, then at the huge gorillas. Paul was fascinated by the timber wolves, while I liked the children's zoo the best. That was where they kept the baby animals, and you could walk around among them and pet everything from soft baby llamas to tiny yellow chicks.

At last, completely exhausted, we collapsed on a bench near the pink flamingo sanctuary.

"We must have walked for miles," Paul said as he removed his shoes and stretched his feet out in front of him. "And we haven't even seen all of it yet."

"We could come here for three Sundays and still not see it all," I told him. I looked around at the families with their children, and at the teenagers walking around. Some were doing the same thing as Paul and I—just enjoying the sights. But some were working, running the food stands or cleaning up the litter. A lucky few even got to tend the animals.

"I tried to get a job here last summer," I said. "I filled out an application, then walked around in a daze for a week, hoping they'd call me. From what I understand they get hundreds of applications every summer, but only hire a few dozen part-timers. They didn't call me."

"Too bad. It'd be a fun job."

"It sure would. I might try again next summer. I do know for sure that I don't want to work at the Dairy Delight again. Being around all that ice cream was bad for my complexion. Chocolate is my favorite."

"Maybe you could get a job at Jessup's," he suggested.

"Do you think I could?" It didn't sound like such a bad idea. "I'm saving my money for a car. I have almost five hundred dollars already, from my job last summer and the baby-sitting I sometimes do during the winter. My father says that if I can save a thousand dollars he'll help

me pick out a good car and he'll make up the
difference. I suspect he said that because he
thought I'd never be able to save that much
money, but I'm going to surprise him and then
he'll have to stick to his end of the bargain.''

The sun was beginning to set when Paul and
I decided to head back home. The ride back
seemed endless, probably because we were tired
out from exploring the zoo.

''Are your parents expecting you home any
special time?'' he asked, riding along beside me.

''No, I told them I might be late. Why?''

''When I was in the mall this week filling out
applications I found out that there's a place
called Below Ground, where they have dances
every Saturday and Sunday night.''

I let my bike coast along on the downgrade,
to give my legs a rest. ''Yes, I know. It's in the
basement of the mall. Daphne and I used to go
once in a while.''

''Do you want to stop there for a little
while?'' he asked. ''We'll be passing right by the
mall on our way home.''

''You mean *now*?'' I didn't know where he
got his energy, but my supply had just about run
out.

''Sure. Why not?'' He grinned.

"Okay, but it'll probably be the death of me. Paul, my legs are about to fall off as it is. If I dance I'll probably end up in a wheelchair."

He coasted along beside me. "We don't have to dance if you don't want to. We could just sit and enjoy the music. It'll give us a chance to rest a bit before going the rest of the way home."

"But I'm not dressed for a dance," I pointed out. "And my hair is windblown and I look awful."

"You look terrific," he said. I felt myself blushing. "Anyhow, who cares? We'll have fun."

"All right," I agreed. "But just for a little while, okay? We play volleyball in gym tomorrow, and I'm going to be so stiff they'll think I'm my seventy-year-old grandmother."

Sunday evening at Below Ground wasn't nearly as busy as Saturday nights were, and we found a booth easily.

"You know what you look like?" Paul asked after ordering a couple of Cokes.

"I'm afraid to guess."

"You look like one of those fuzzy little koala bears we saw at the zoo."

"Oh, great," I said. "I've always wanted to look like an Australian animal."

Paul laughed and put his hand over mine on the table. "I thought they were cute."

There was a deejay playing music on an elaborate stereo system, and a few couples were dancing in the middle of the dance floor. It was a slow number.

"Let's dance," Paul said.

"Oh, no, really—"

He pulled me to my feet before I could protest any more and had me out on the dance floor so quickly that I wasn't sure how we'd gotten there.

Paul wrapped his arms around me and I found myself holding on to his shoulders, moving to the rhythm of the music.

And I had thought Paul was shy! I was beginning to feel that perhaps I was the shy one.

"Hi, Marcy."

I looked up and saw Dot Van Atta dancing just a few feet away with a boy who looked vaguely familiar.

"Hi," I said. "Uh—you know Paul, don't you? Paul, this is Dot Van Atta."

"Sure, Dot's in my algebra class," Paul said.

Dot was looking at us curiously, and I knew she was dying to know how I knew Paul. I didn't feel like going into explanations, so I maneuvered Paul away to the other side of the dance floor.

"How come you never go to any of the games, or any other school activities?" I asked abruptly. "It's a great way to meet people."

"I already told you," he said. "I have to work. And when we moved here I found that La Mesa High was slightly ahead of my old school, which meant that I had to study extra hard to catch up."

"Mr. Kirkpatrick told me you were one of his best students."

"I worked at it, and he knew it. I'm just about caught up now. It's only lately that I've been able to relax a little and have some time to myself. When I started looking around and noticing my surroundings, the first thing I noticed was you."

Just as things were really starting to get interesting, the song ended and the deejay announced that he was taking a break. I was disappointed, and even more so when Paul suggested that maybe it was time to head for home. He'd had to talk me into going there in the first place, but now that we were there I wanted to stay. Dot waved to us as we walked out the door.

We only had a couple of miles to go, so it didn't take long to get to my house. As we rounded the last corner, Paul caught up and rode beside me.

"This has been about the nicest day I've had since I moved here," he said.

I smiled. "Would you like to come inside and have some lemonade before you go home?" I asked.

"I don't think that's such a good idea," he said.

I followed the direction of his gaze. Clay's car was parked in the driveway!

Chapter Nine

Oh, Marcy," Mom said when she saw me, "I'm so glad you're back. Clay and I were just talking about our camping trip. Clay thinks it sounds great. I wish you and your sister would show as much enthusiasm about this whole thing." She gave me a nervous look. "I asked Clay to join us."

Mom meant well, so I couldn't be mad at her, but at that moment I sincerely wished she hadn't said anything to Clay about the trip.

I sat down beside him and looked at the map

that was spread out across the kitchen table. "Have you ever been camping before?" I asked.

"Sure, lots of times," Clay said. "When I was a kid I used to go to camp every summer, and we always spent a night or two out in the wilds in our sleeping bags. We used to scare each other half to death with ghost stories. It was terrific!"

B.J. came into the room and sat across from me. I was glad to have her there. She was the only one who knew what I was going through.

"Clay brought some papers for you," my mother said, "so I asked him in. I figured you'd be home soon." She stood up. "And now I have a ton of bookkeeping to do. It was nice talking to you, Clay. I'll see you next weekend."

"You brought some papers for me?" I asked Clay.

"Oh, yeah." He reached across the table and picked up a stack of papers I hadn't noticed. "I ended up making a few changes on that report."

I looked down at my neatly typewritten pages and saw that he had inked instructions here and there and had crossed out some lines. All my work for nothing!

"Now it needs to be typed all over again," he said. He took a sip from the glass of lemonade beside him.

I heard B.J. make a little choking sound beside me, and I kicked her under the table to stop the remark I knew was coming.

"Yes, I can see that it'll have to be retyped," I said calmly.

B.J. tensed beside me, and I gave her arm a little squeeze. She clammed up, but I could tell it was an effort for her.

Leaving Clay and B.J. in the kitchen, I stomped upstairs, then down again.

"Here you go," I said, handing my typewriter to Clay.

He looked at the machine with astonishment.

"The *s* key sticks just a little bit," I told him. "There's plenty of paper there for your report. I'll need it back by Thursday because I have some work of my own to do."

I walked a stunned Clay to the front door. "Couldn't you—" he said at the last minute.

I shook my head. "I'm too tired to do it tonight, Clay. And since you need it tomorrow morning you'll have to do it yourself."

He must have sensed my determination because he didn't try to change my mind.

B.J. let out a whoop when I came back into the kitchen a minute later. "There's hope for you after all," she said. "I was beginning to have my doubts."

Mr. Kirkpatrick, after his initial surprise, accepted Paul's new job as part of the experiment. He even congratulated him in front of the whole class for his initiative.

We were sure to get an A on this experiment, and I knew I had Paul to thank.

Daphne turned around in her seat. "Looks like you were pretty lucky to get Paul, after all," she whispered. "Hank, on the other hand, may be a whiz at chess, but his economics leaves a lot to be desired. And I made a real mistake by going out with him a couple of times. Now he won't leave me alone."

"You looked as though you were having a good time the night of the bonfire," I said in a low voice.

"I was. But that doesn't mean I'm ready to be tied down to one boy. You know what I mean, all right. Dot told me this morning about you and Paul."

Naturally. Dot had told her she'd seen me at the dance with Paul. But Daphne didn't seem to think there was anything odd about it. She was always juggling two and sometimes three guys at a time, and she just figured that I was doing the same. Well, maybe I was, but I didn't feel too good about it.

It was funny about this new group of friends I'd acquired since I'd first started going out with Clay. For a long time I'd watched them with envy and wished I could be one of them. They were all so attractive and well dressed, and whenever you looked at them they appeared to be having a good time. They seemed special somehow, almost like celebrities.

Daphne had always been a part of that crowd. She was just the type to be popular. For a long time she'd been trying to persuade me to overcome my shyness. She'd painted a glowing picture of what life would be like for me if only I would move in the right circles. Gradually I'd come to believe her and I'd made a real effort to socialize. Then Clay had asked me out, and all of a sudden the miracle had happened. Now all I had to do was to figure out why I wasn't happier about it.

For one thing, I'd discovered that they weren't that different from anyone else. They all worried about the same old things that had always bothered me—grades, parents, dates, the future. I'd even come to the conclusion that

Chelsea Fisher, Clay's old girlfriend, wasn't as bad as I'd imagined. The first couple of times that I'd gone out with Clay, I'd seen her practically everywhere. I was sure that she resented me for being with him. I'd even imagined dirty looks and the cold shoulder.

I was constantly on edge, expecting her to make a big play to get him back. But this never happened—at least not that I heard about. After a while I began to see her with a good-looking boy who I heard was a freshman in college. Not only did she seem disinterested in Clay, she'd obviously found someone she liked better.

One more thing. I was beginning to wonder if I liked Clay that much myself. I had the distinct feeling that he was using me. And I didn't like it. Not one bit. I was also finding myself becoming fonder of Paul, who had biked quickly away when he'd seen Clay's car in our driveway, and had not even cast a glance my way, and now wasn't even talking to me in school.

I began to daydream about him in class. In p.e. my coordination deserted me. At volleyball I kept missing the shots, and my serves wouldn't even go over the net.

"Come on, Marcy," Juliet Adams complained. "If you can't keep up today, then sit out and give the team a chance." Juliet took her sports seriously. She really hated to lose.

Forcing a smile, I said, "Maybe I will sit out the next game. I'm a little tired today."

"Sure she's tired." Toni Sheldon laughed, poking her sister Carrie in the ribs. "Out with Clay on Saturday night and Paul on Sunday night, she *should* be tired. How do you do it, Marcy?"

I just smiled mysteriously at them and went to sit on the bleachers. As soon as a new game began they all lost interest in me again, and I pulled my knees up and wrapped my arms around my legs. I rested my chin on my knees, and my eyes followed the game without really seeing it.

So, the news of my busy weekend was all over the school! Lots of girls went out with more than one boy at a time. Usually that wouldn't generate this much interest, but several factors made my case a hot item.

First of all, Clay was one of the most popular boys in the school, and when a girl was lucky enough to be asked out by him she didn't risk blowing it by playing the field.

Also, everyone knew that I hadn't done much dating before Clay, so the fact that I now seemed to have *two* boyfriends was enough to make everyone wonder what had happened to change quiet little Marcy, the class brain who used to go steady with her books.

But I didn't have two boyfriends. Not really. And the way things were going today it was very possible that neither Clay nor Paul would want to go out with me again. Clay was obviously put out because I'd made him do his own typing instead of jumping at the chance to do it for him. Just how badly put out, only time would tell. And now Paul seemed to be avoiding me. He'd known all along that I was going out with Clay, and he'd never said anything about wanting me to stop. Yet why had he been so distant in class? He'd seemed so friendly yesterday at the zoo.

I blinked as I realized that Daphne was waving her hand in front of my face.

"Marcy, didn't you hear the bell?" she asked. "It's time to shower and get ready for our next class."

The volleyball game had ended and I hadn't even noticed. I followed her out of the gym.

"Guess what?" she said. "I think I've finally talked my father into letting me get a car. I gave him the old 'things have changed since you were a kid' speech. I explained to him that girls these days aren't dependent on guys to drive them around everywhere. I *need* a car, I told him. He seems to be softening on the idea a bit. I think he just hates to face the fact that I'm growing up, but he's going to have to get used to the idea sooner or later."

"Do you want to go shopping with me after school today?" I asked as we reached the locker room. "My mother and I are going to the mall to check out the sales."

Daphne pulled her T-shirt off over her head. "I don't know. Toni Sheldon said something about looking through the catalogs for new cheerleading outfits. The outfits we have now are getting pretty worn, and we're trying to come up with some fund-raising ideas."

"Couldn't you do that some other time?" I asked. "We haven't been shopping together in a long time."

"That's true." She picked up a towel and draped it across the back of her neck. "But we can always go shopping this weekend, if nothing else comes up. The sales will still be going on. I'm kind of anxious to pick out the new outfits."

"Okay." I sighed. "We can do it some other time."

Mom was waiting for me outside the school at three-thirty. I climbed in the car and threw my books in the back seat.

"Couldn't Daphne come?" she asked.

"She had better things to do."

"That's too bad," Mom said. "But we'll have a good time, just the two of us. It'll be just like old times."

Nothing's just like old times, I thought unhappily. *Everything's changing.*

Chapter Ten

The stores in the mall were having their Crazy Days Sales, so it was wall-to-wall people wherever we went. Mom bought me a couple of pairs of jeans in Maurice's clothing store, and she found a sweater for herself in Boston's.

In Jessup's we explored the sale racks, but I couldn't stop thinking that Paul was around somewhere. This was his first day on his new job, and I was afraid that any minute we'd run into him. I didn't know if I was ready for that.

He showed up just as Mom was paying for a new nightgown for B.J.

"Hi, Marcy," he said, setting down the two small boxes he'd been carrying. He was wearing a starched brown uniform shirt that said Jessup's over the left pocket.

I introduced him to my mother, who greeted him and then suddenly remembered a housecoat she'd seen on a rack and simply had to take another look at. The next thing I knew, I was standing in the middle of the crowded department store facing Paul.

"How's the first day on the job?" I asked.

"Not bad. I think I'm going to like it here. The people are friendly. Would you like a tour?"

"Can you do that?" I asked. I looked down at the boxes he'd been carrying.

"I'm on my break right now," he explained. "I was just going to drop these off in advertising on my way to the lounge. Come on, I'll show you around."

I was so relieved that he no longer seemed angry with me that I followed him without stopping to think that my mother might wonder where I'd disappeared to.

It felt strange going through the double doors marked Employees Only and following Paul down the wide corridors. At a door marked

Advertising he knocked once, then pushed the door open.

A slender, gray-haired woman was seated on a high stool, a pencil propped over one ear.

"Here are the pictures you needed, Mrs. Baker," Paul said, setting down the boxes on top of a metal file cabinet. "This is Marcy, a friend of mine from school."

Mrs. Baker took off her glasses and placed them on the slanted table she'd been working at.

A man in a brown shirt just like Paul's stuck his head in the door. "Paul," he said, "can you give me a hand for a minute? I've got to get one of those new stereos down from the top shelf in the back room."

Paul looked inquiringly at me.

"Go ahead, Paul," Mrs. Baker said. "Marcy can wait here with me until you're done."

"Thanks," he told her. Then he winked at me and said, "I'll just be a couple of minutes."

"This seems to be a busy store," I said when Mrs. Baker and I were alone in the room.

"It is," she said. "That's what I like about it. Are you interested in advertising, Marcy?"

"I don't know. I don't know very much about it."

Mrs. Baker picked up a large piece of lined paper. "This is next week's ad," she explained.

"These big boxes here are filled with pictures of clothing, sporting goods and everything else we carry in the store. I'll find the pictures for the ad and arrange them on the paper. Then I'll fill in the regular and sale prices, the dates of the sale and whatever else we need. I'll paste everything onto the paper before taking it down to the newspaper office. They'll print it up and it'll appear in Saturday's edition, on the back page."

It took Paul nearly fifteen minutes to get back, and by then I was totally caught up in what Mrs. Baker was telling me. She'd let me make up some sample ad pages myself, then she'd pointed out the importance of composition and balance. I was so absorbed in what we were doing that I didn't even hear Paul come into the room.

"Sorry I took so long," he said. "We had to move several boxes out of the way before we could get to the stereo."

"Oh, that's okay. Mrs. Baker was showing me all about advertising."

"I was showing you a *little bit* about advertising," she corrected. "This is just the tip of the iceberg. We also do radio and television spots, magazine ads—"

"Could I come back sometime?" I asked. I knew I had to get back to my mother, who was probably about ready to call out the National Guard by now, but I was so fascinated by what Mrs. Baker was showing me that I knew I had to learn more.

Mrs. Baker looked at Paul, then shrugged. "Certainly you may come back, if you want to. I'm here every day. And if you're really that interested in it, you might want to go down to Personnel and fill out an application. During the summer months we hire quite a few teenagers to help out with the extra load."

I wanted to hug her. But I also wanted to appear as sophisticated and mature as possible, so I kept the impulse to myself.

Mom was pacing near the purse and belt section when I found her a few minutes later. I explained what had kept me so long. My enthusiasm was so obvious that she didn't mind that I'd kept her waiting.

I went back to Jessup's the very next day, right after school. Paul didn't look surprised to see me. He knew that I tended to throw myself headlong into whatever interested me.

Mrs. Baker didn't seem to mind having me hang around, so I really took advantage of her good nature and by the end of the week she was letting me help set ads and run errands for her. Since the personnel director had made it clear to me that they were through hiring part-timers until school let out in the spring, I was grateful to Mrs. Baker for letting me hang around.

"The best part," I told B.J. as we gave our bedroom its mandatory weekly cleaning, "is that when summer comes I'll already have all this experience in the advertising department, so they'll just about have to place me there."

"*If* they decide to hire you," B.J. said, leaning over to strip the sheets from her bed.

"They *will* hire me," I said firmly. "Mrs. Baker said she'll put in a good word for me. That'll have to count for something. She's pretty important around there. And besides, with her teaching me the department, and all I'm learning about the store, I wouldn't have to go through the usual training period. They'd be crazy *not* to hire me."

"You want that job pretty badly, don't you?" B.J. observed.

"It's the first time I've ever been eager to go to work." I threw our sheets in a laundry basket, then pulled all the clothes out of our hamper and threw them on top of the sheets. "It never gets boring around there. Mrs. Baker says she's been there for almost thirteen years and she still loves it.''

B.J. took one handle of the laundry basket and I took the other and together we carried it to the utility room. While I sorted out the bright colors and delicate items, B.J. measured the detergent.

"I'm surprised Mom has let you spend so much time at Jessup's this week," B.J. said. She dumped the detergent into the washing machine and turned the dial to cold water wash. "She's always said she wouldn't let you have a job during the school year because it might interfere with your studies. Even Dad hasn't said anything about it yet."

I'd wondered myself why neither of them had said anything about all the after-school hours I'd been spending at Jessup's. Maybe it was because they were both busy getting ready for our camping trip, which was a mere two days away.

That was another problem. Did Clay still plan on going with us? I hadn't heard anything to the contrary. I wasn't at all sure I liked the idea. Although I hadn't seen much of Paul all week— at school he was wrapped up studying for an important biology test and at Jessup's he was usually in the stockroom—I still thought about him a lot and found myself wondering if I was letting something special slip between my fingers. Paul wasn't the pushy type. I had the feeling he was keeping his distance to give me the time to think about what I wanted. The trouble was I didn't know. Every time I thought about either Clay or Paul, I felt confused. Boys! I had been better off without them in the old days, when Daphne and I had been best friends. Now I hardly ever saw her anymore.

"There," B.J. said, closing the lid of the washing machine. "If you can pull yourself out of your trance, you could carry the vacuum cleaner to our room. Gee, remember when we were little and we didn't have to do any of this stuff? How come it's not like that anymore?"

I dragged the vacuum cleaner out of the utility room closet and started for our room. "It's called growing up, B.J.," I said. "And I'm not sure, either, that it's such a hot idea."

Chapter Eleven

On Friday, Clay caught up with me just as I was leaving school.

"Well," he said, "tomorrow's the big day! It's supposed to be chilly over the weekend, so I've packed loads of warm clothes. My father wasn't too crazy about the idea at first, but I convinced him that it would be all healthy outdoor stuff and that we'd be back at a reasonable hour Sunday night."

"Yeh, I know. He called. I could hear my father giving him the old pitch."

"He did? You could? I wonder why? Why do parents always feel that they have to check up every little thing you do?"

"Who knows?" I was beginning to dread the whole idea and having Clay around meant just one more thing to have to deal with. "Maybe he thought I had designs on you. You know, a camping trip sounds kind of wild, though if only they knew my parents! It's all the rugged life for them, not much time for fun and games, if you know what I mean. And to top it all, we have to make an early start; five-thirty in the morning." I groaned. "I haven't been up that early since sixth grade when Daphne and I spent the entire night listening to rock albums."

"Oh, well," said Clay. "I don't really mind. I often get up early to work out."

That settled that. I hadn't discouraged him at all. I walked slowly home, trying to forget the happy days in the wilderness with up-and-at-em Clay that lay ahead.

At the top of the hill near our house I could already see the van parked in our driveway. Mom was loading the gear.

"Marcy, what kept you?" she asked when she saw me.

"School got out fifteen minutes ago," I said. "It takes me that long to walk home."

"But B.J.'s been home for half an hour already."

"That's because the junior high gets out half an hour earlier than the senior high."

Mom picked up the cooler, which was dented on one corner but still usable. "Will you take this to the kitchen and rinse it out with vinegar and water? It smells a little musty." She handed it to me. "And tell your father that I found his binoculars here in the garage. He's probably tearing the house apart looking for them."

I carried the cooler to the kitchen and put it down on the counter. After changing out of my school clothes I went looking for Dad. I found him in his bedroom, the entire contents of his closet spread out on the carpet.

"Mom says to tell you she found your binoculars in the garage," I said.

He just looked at the mess around him. "Terrific," he said with a sigh.

While Mom and Dad were fussing around trying to get ready, B.J. was amazingly well organized. She had finished all her packing by the time I'd cleaned out the cooler, and had even started on mine.

"You won't believe this," she told me, "but I'm starting to look forward to this trip. Just a little bit. The city is getting a little boring.

Maybe we'll see something interesting in the mountains.''

"Like a grizzly bear," I snapped. What had happened to my most dependable ally? The one person I'd always depended on to hate camping as much as I did?

"You know there aren't really any grizzly bears there. There aren't any mountain lions, either. The wildest thing we'll probably see all weekend will be Mom's hair without her curling iron.''

"Where's my La Mesa High sweatshirt?" I said, pushing aside the clothes in the bottom drawer of my dresser.

B.J. handed me my half-filled canvas suitcase. "I already packed it. I knew you'd want to take it. Is Clay still planning to come along?''

"I guess so.''

"I think it's kind of a romantic idea." She sighed. "You'll be able to look at the stars together, and go for walks in the mountains. I can't wait until Mom and Dad let me start dating, and I can invite someone along on a weekend like this.''

I tried to ignore her as I threw some underwear and socks into my bag.

"Too bad it isn't Paul you're taking," she remarked.

"What?" I stopped what I was doing and straightened up to look at her. "What did you say?"

"Nothing," B.J. said.

"Yes you did," I insisted. "You said—"

The phone rang then and B.J. pounced on it. After speaking briefly, she held it out to me. "Daphne," she said.

I took the phone from B.J.

"Marcy, are you coming to the game tonight?" Daphne asked. "I looked around for you after school, but you were already gone. It's a big game tonight. We play Kearny High, and they're the ones who swore they'd get even with us for knocking them out of the sectionals last year. And Josh Frankel has a sprained wrist so a lot of pressure will be on Clay to play his best."

"I can't tonight. I have too much to do around here. I'd forgotten we were scheduled to play Kearny, but it wouldn't have mattered anyway because Mom already said I had to stay home tonight and go to bed early so I can get up at the most awful hour."

"Sounds gruesome. Couldn't you get out for just a little while? A whole bunch of us are going to go out for Cokes after the game. You wouldn't want to miss that, would you?"

I wasn't sure. A month ago I would have been happy to be included in the group, but somehow it didn't seem quite as important to me anymore.

"Just can't," I said. "This is the weekend I told you about, remember? We're going camping. Clay is coming along, so he'll be going straight home after the game, anyway."

"Gee, I'm not so sure," Daphne said.

"What do you mean?"

"Well, I'm positive I heard him tell a couple of the guys that he'd just gassed up his car so he could drive them to McDonald's after the game. Maybe he forgot that this is the weekend he's going with you. Do you want me to remind him when I see him at the game?"

"No, don't do that," I said. "He didn't forget, because I just talked to him about it a while ago. I guess losing sleep doesn't bother him."

"Don't worry too much about it," Daphne advised. "I'm sure he won't stay out late."

After I'd hung up the phone I sat on my bed for a little while feeling hurt. Clay didn't even care enough about this camping trip to give up one night out with his buddies. It wasn't going to be much of a weekend if he was too tired to enjoy it.

"Do you have any film in your camera?" B.J. asked from across the room. "I think I have an extra roll around somewhere if you need it."

"Hmm?" I looked up at her. "Oh, yeah, I have plenty of film." I tried to remember what it was we'd been talking about before Daphne had called. Then I remembered. "Hey, what was it you were saying a few minutes ago?" I asked.

B.J. arranged her face in a look of total innocence. "Saying? I wasn't saying anything at all."

I jumped up from the bed and caught her just as she tried to get to the bedroom door. Laughing, she ducked out of my reach and fell across her bed. I landed on top of her and held her there. I was giggling myself by then, because she was making the most ridiculous faces at me.

"Now tell me," I said, pinning her arms down. "You said it was too bad I wasn't taking Paul, didn't you?"

B.J. shook her head from side to side and refused to say anything.

Holding her down with the weight of my body, I began to tickle her ribs with my fingers. B.J. is the most ticklish person in the world. I hadn't done it in years, but when we were both kids I used to tickle her every once in a while.

She was a lot stronger now, though, and I had a lot of trouble keeping her down.

Finally she exploded with laughter, her face bright red from holding it in. "Okay!" she shrieked. "I admit it. I *do* wish you were taking Paul this weekend instead of Clay."

I let her go and collapsed beside her on the bed. We lay there side by side, catching our breath and staring up at the ceiling. I felt a thousand percent better than I had just a minute before, after my conversation with Daphne.

"You still like Paul the best, huh?" I said when I was able to speak.

"Oh, sure. I think he's great. I also think he's not going to let you string him along forever, and when he gets tired of waiting for you to come to your senses he's going to start looking around for someone else. I may be only fourteen now, and too young for Paul, but in a few more years three years' difference won't be that much. When I'm eighteen and Paul is twenty-one I *won't* be too young for him. And I'm going to make sure he knows I'm around."

I propped myself up on one elbow so that I could see her face. All of a sudden my little sister didn't look so little anymore. "Are you saying you'd try to take Paul from me?" I asked.

"Of course not," B.J. said. "If you and Paul were going together I'd be the first one to wish you both the best. I think you and Paul make a much better couple than you and Clay. All I'm saying is that if it doesn't work out between you and Paul I wouldn't mind having a shot at him myself."

"He's a guy, B.J.," I said, "not a deer during hunting season. And to tell you the truth, I wish he was coming this weekend, too." I sat up and swung my legs over the side of her bed. "I think that after this weekend I'll tell Clay that it would be best if we didn't date anymore. How do I tell him? Do I have to do it face-to-face, or can I write him a letter? I've never done this sort of thing before. I'm not sure how it's done."

"I think you should definitely tell him face-to-face," she told me. "A letter seems sort of chicken."

"I suppose you're right."

"When did you make up your mind?"

"When Daphne told me that Clay was planning to go out tonight after the game," I said. To Clay I was just another name on the long list of girls he'd gone with. He wouldn't be devastated when I broke up with him. He probably wouldn't care much at all.

There was a knock on our door then and Dad's voice called, "Supper's ready, girls."

The next morning we were all up and about by a little after five. Since B.J. and I had gone to bed very early, we didn't have too much trouble adjusting to the early hour. I was worried, however, that Clay might oversleep and hold things up. Not that I cared if this trip was delayed, but I knew my folks would be annoyed if he kept us waiting.

He wasn't late, though. Promptly at five-thirty he knocked on the front door. I opened the door, then immediately bent to scoop up the weekend edition of the Le Mesa Shopper.

"It's here," I said excitedly. Quickly I snapped the rubber band off the rolled-up paper and opened it to look for Jessup's ad.

"You aren't exactly going to have much time for shopping this weekend," Clay said as he followed me inside.

I found Jessup's full-page ad and showed it to him. "I helped design this ad," I told him.

"Good morning, Clay," my mother said, walking past us with an armful of paper plates and cups. "Marcy, show Clay where to put his things. I saved a place near the back of the van."

My eyes were still on the ad, which seemed to me to be the most beautiful thing I'd ever seen. I wanted to tell the world about it. I felt as proud as though I'd done it all myself, rather than just a part of it.

"That's real nice," Clay said, but I could tell he wasn't really interested. "You want to show me where to put my stuff now? I'll get this put away and then I can ask your father if he needs help with anything."

Hiding my disappointment, I started to fold up the paper. Later I'd cut out the ad and put it in my scrapbook.

But before I closed the paper B.J. appeared and snatched it from my hands. "Is this the one?" she asked. "You're famous! My sister the advertising tycoon. Are you going to keep it? You should have it framed and hang it on the wall in our bedroom. I think I'll pick up a paper for myself, then I can show it to everyone at school. Too bad they didn't put your name on it anywhere. Some of those creeps at school probably won't believe me when I tell them you did this ad, but my friends will believe me. Oh, hi, Clay."

B.J.'s enthusiasm was exactly what I needed. I felt good again. "You can have that one," I told her. "I'll get another for myself."

"Thanks!"

Clay frowned and looked at the ad again. "What's the big deal?" he asked. "You said you only helped with the ad, you didn't do it yourself."

B.J. glared at him as she rolled up the paper and held it protectively against her chest. "Next time your basketball team wins an important game I'll remind you that you only *helped*, and that you didn't do it yourself."

"What's with her?" Clay asked as B.J. stomped off to our room.

"She's very loyal," I said. "Unlike some people I know."

"Huh?"

"How was the game last night? Did we win?"

He brightened. "By eight points. They were ahead all the way through the first three quarters, then, just when they started feeling over-confident, we moved in and ran right over them. You should have seen them. They were so mad that we half expected some of them to be waiting for us after we left the gym. But I guess they cooled off because there wasn't any trouble after all."

I took Clay outside to the van and helped him squeeze in his things. The van was so full you'd have thought we were planning to be away a month.

"Did you do anything after the game?" I asked casually. Maybe he'd tell me he'd gone straight home after all.

"Oh, sure," he said. "It wouldn't have been much of a celebration if we didn't go out afterward. A bunch of us went to McDonald's and stayed so long that I almost didn't make it home in time for curfew. I made it, though, and it's a good thing. The coach would have benched me if I'd broken training and he found out about it. I had a heck of a time getting out of bed when the alarm went off this morning."

"I can imagine."

Even though I'd already decided that Clay and I weren't meant for each other, I was still annoyed that he'd gone out without even thinking about me.

After B.J. took her kitten to the neighbors' house where it was going to spend the weekend, we all got in the van. Mom and Dad sat in front, with B.J., Clay and me sharing the seat that went lengthwise from right behind Dad's seat to the back of the van.

"Here we go," Dad called cheerfully as he backed the van out of the driveway.

"Yay," B.J. shouted. She was really getting into the mood of this thing.

Me? I was busy figuring out in my head that it would be about forty hours before I'd be back to the comfort of my own soft bed.

Chapter Twelve

It took only a couple of hours to reach the Sheep Hole Mountains, and from there it was an uphill drive.

"Marcy, look at that breathtaking view," Mom said for about the tenth time.

"It sure is a long way down," B.J. said.

I pointed my face toward the window so Mom would think I was looking, but my eyes were firmly shut. If I looked I just knew I would be sick.

"Hey, you're cheating," Clay said.

I poked him in the ribs with my elbow.

Fortunately, Dad got off the main road before too long and began looking for a campsite. B.J. and I weren't too picky, but Mom had her heart set on setting up camp beside a stream. As soon as we found a spot where camping wasn't prohibited, Dad pulled the van to a halt and jumped out.

"How's this?" he asked, looking around.

"I don't know," Mom said.

"It's perfect," he insisted. "Beautiful scenery, lush trees, the required babbling brook. What more could you want?"

"Aren't we a little far from civilization?" I asked. "Couldn't we find a campsite with some other people?"

Dad walked to the edge of the stream and bent to dip his fingers in the water. "The whole idea of this weekend is to get *away* from civilization."

"I like it here," B.J. announced. She had opened a bag of chips and was munching. "It reminds me of that movie I saw last month, *Friday the Thirteenth, Part Three.*"

"That's the one that gave you nightmares," I reminded her.

"You were afraid to even go see it," Clay reminded me.

"I don't like that kind of movie."

"I think this spot will be fine," Mom finally decided.

Dad and Clay unpacked the van and set up the extralarge tent Dad had bought. B.J. unpacked the food, and Mom and I gathered firewood and arranged stones in a small circle in the middle of the clearing. Dad had brought fishing poles and had big plans for our catching our own supper.

"There are trails all through these woods," Clay told me once the tent was up. "I walked just a little ways down that one there." He pointed toward the trees. I didn't see any trail. "I only went a few feet before I couldn't even hear you all anymore. The trees really block the sound. Do you want to go explore?"

"I think Mom wants me to help her with the folding table and chairs," I said.

Mom stuck her head out from inside the van. "You two go ahead," she said. "B.J. can help me with this stuff."

Even though I had decided ahead of time that I wasn't going to like this outing, I had to admit that it was a pretty spot. The sun was high, but when we walked along the trail the trees nearly blocked it out, making everything cool and green. I zipped up my jacket, glad that Mom had insisted I bring it along. It was chilly here, and I knew that if we were to go any higher into the mountains we'd very likely find snow.

"Your father brought along some extra rubber hip boots for me so that I can fish," Clay said, pushing aside a branch. "It's a good thing, because that stream is like ice. Funny what a difference just a few miles and a little altitude can make. Down in La Mesa it's the sort of day where you could run around in shirt sleeves, but up here it's cold and I'll bet we get plenty of frost tonight."

We were a little way from the campsite now, and it worried me that we couldn't hear anything other than the usual wildlife noises. I looked behind me at the trail we'd been walking on. It looked very narrow and nearly grown over.

"Maybe we should head back," I suggested.

"Sure," he said. "Your father says he brought along a small kerosene heater that he'll use for a little while tonight to warm up the inside of the tent. He won't let it run all night, though, because that might not be safe."

We had turned and were walking back in the direction of the campsite. I sighed in relief when I heard B.J.'s loud and comforting voice in the distance.

"It'll get cold, too," I told Clay, thinking about what he'd said about Dad not letting the heater run all night. "We've been on these winter camping trips before. I usually end up sleeping ducked down all the way in my sleeping bag, with about three pairs of socks on my feet."

When we got back to the campsite I helped Mom fix lunch while Dad, Clay and B.J. explored some more. I could have gone with them, because Mom had told me there wasn't much to do and she could handle it herself, but I didn't want to wander around in strange woods anymore. I longed for city lights and other signs of civilization. We couldn't even get anything on the van's radio, because of the surrounding hills.

After lunch we played with the Frisbee, then we all took turns fishing. Clay caught two, and B.J. caught one that was so small she felt sorry for it and threw it back. Mom and I didn't have any luck at all, and Dad got several nibbles but they kept getting away from him.

"Yuck," B.J. said, looking at the two large fish Clay held up proudly. "Are we really going to *eat* them?"

"You love fish, B.J.," Mom reminded her.

"Not when they have eyes that keep looking at me."

However, she changed her mind after Mom panfried them, and she ate as much as anyone else. The sun was beginning to go down by the time we finished, so Dad set up a few battery-powered lanterns around the tent.

Mom and Dad were sitting side by side on a big rock by the stream; Dad had his arm across her shoulders. B.J. was huddled close to a lantern, reading a magazine. Clay and I sat looking into the dying embers of the campfire.

"It sure is quiet up here," Clay said.

"That's what my parents like about it," I told him. "It hasn't been as bad as I thought it was going to be. I haven't seen any wild animals yet and I haven't even been bored."

"That's because you've been with me."

I looked up and caught his grin. "This is a far cry from the way you usually spend your Saturday nights," I said. "No regrets?"

"No regrets. Want to go for a walk again?" His hand slipped out of the pocket of his jacket and held mine.

I reminded myself that I'd made a decision about the relationship between Clay and myself, and I shook my head. "Dad doesn't want us to leave the campsite after sundown. It's too easy to get lost up here."

"Tomorrow?"

"Okay." I nodded. "Tomorrow."

All five of us slept in the tent that night. The tent was big enough that we weren't crowded, and our combined body heat kept us fairly comfortable. I was a little stiff in the morning, but I soon walked the kinks out and was even looking forward to exploring a bit more.

"Be back by lunchtime," Dad said as Clay and I prepared to walk along a new trail.

"We will," I promised.

We walked in the opposite direction from where we'd gone the day before. This path took us slightly uphill, and after a while the way seemed to be getting a little rough.

"Whew. Maybe we picked the wrong trail this time," I said. "I'm getting tired already."

"I think there's a clearing ahead. Let's go on a little farther. We can rest there, then head back." He walked on ahead, and I had no choice but to follow. His long legs covered ground easily, but I had to hurry to keep up.

"Hey!" Clay stopped so suddenly that I nearly smacked into his back.

"What is it?" I asked.

He stepped aside and I saw a clearing just ahead. A morning mist hung heavily in the air, making everything seem hazy, like a photograph that was slightly out of focus.

There was a cliff there—not very steep, but it overlooked a deep valley. It was a beautiful spot, and so peaceful that I could almost imagine that no one else had ever seen it.

"This is really something," Clay whispered after a while.

"It sure is," I whispered back. I wasn't sure *why* we were whispering, but it somehow seemed appropriate. "It looks like something out of a movie."

We sat on a patch of soft grass and just looked at the scenery before us. The sun rose higher in the sky and the mist began to evaporate slowly, although it still stayed chilly. Small animals scurried about, but they didn't bother me in the least.

"This is nice," Clay said. "We should come back here this spring and see what it looks like when the flowers begin to bloom."

Clunk. The perfection of the morning was shattered. Clay's words reminded me that—for us anyway—there would be no more camping trips.

"Why did you go to McDonald's Friday night?" I blurted out. I hadn't meant to ask this so bluntly, but it had been nagging at me. "I thought you'd go home right after the game, since I wasn't able to go out with you."

"I always go out after the game Friday nights. It's a tradition. You know that."

"I thought that when two people were supposedly going together they wouldn't *want* to go out without each other."

"Is that why you were at the Below Ground dance with Paul Ryan last Sunday night?"

He had me there, all right.

"If you knew about that, why didn't you say anything about it all week?" I asked. "Didn't you care?"

"Sure I cared. But we aren't going steady, Marcy. I'm not going to tell you what you can or can't do when you're not with me. And that works both ways, of course."

"Of course. We're both free to do exactly what we want. Then why do we even bother with each other? It all seems like a big waste of time to me." I glared at him. "Or did you only take me out so I'd help you with your stupid papers?"

He glared back. "I think I'm the one who was doing the favor. It didn't hurt your reputation any for you to be seen going out with me."

Why, that conceited pig! "Big deal!" I yelled as I got up and hurried away from him.

"Marcy, wait," he called.

I ignored him and walked quickly down the path.

Within minutes Clay caught up with me and grabbed my arm. "Marcy, where are you going? You can't wander around up here."

"I'm not wandering around, I'm going back to the van—away from you." I took a deep breath. "Look, let's just get this camping trip over with, okay?"

Much to my irritation, he continued to hold my arm.

"You're not even headed in the right direction," he said smugly. "The camper is over that way." He pointed back to the direction from which we'd just come.

"No, it isn't," I said. "This is the path we came on. I recognize that tree over there."

"All the trees look alike. You took a wrong turn after you left the clearing."

He might be a jerk, but what if he was right? I followed him back until he stopped and looked around.

"Why did you stop?" I asked.

"Because I think we might have taken another wrong turn," he said.

"You mean you don't know where we are? I thought you were the one who used to go camping all the time as a kid."

"Don't get uptight," he said. "I think we go this way."

"You *think*?"

"I wouldn't have gotten lost in the first place if I hadn't had to go chasing after you," he reminded me.

"Then we *are* lost," I said.

Clay looked around and frowned. "Yeah, we are."

Chapter Thirteen

Clay linked his fingers together so that I could put one foot in the palms of his hands. Then, reaching up as high as I could, I grasped a branch and began to pull myself up the tree.

"I think I'm going to make it," I said as I swung my leg up onto the branch.

It was over three hours since Clay and I had realized we were definitely lost. Clay thought we should stay put and wait for someone to come find us, but I preferred to do something about our situation. The only thing we seemed able to agree upon was that we should stick together.

"If one of us could climb a tall tree, we might be able to spot the campsite," he suggested.

He meant me, natch.

Clay had lifted me, and now I was working my way along the lowest branches of the tree. I refused to look down. I wasn't going to let Clay see that I was a little nervous about doing this.

"Are you okay?" he called.

"Just dandy. I can see over the tops of some of the smaller trees. I see a little smoke coming up in the distance on my left. Do you suppose that's where my parents are?"

"Might be. Can you go any higher?"

"I'll try." I wasn't as nervous now as I'd been at first, and I pulled myself up easily. It was fortunate that I'd worn my comfortable old joggers to hike in. The shoes gripped the bark and kept me from slipping. "Hey," I called, suddenly. "I think I see our camper. We were heading in the wrong direction all along."

A stiff twig slipped out of my hand and smacked me in the face. I'd seen two abandoned birds' nests and had come nose to nose with a hairy green caterpillar, but I felt incredibly good. We could make our way back to the camper now, and it was because I had found it.

It took almost as long to get down as it had to climb up, but finally I felt my feet touch solid ground again.

"It's that way," I told Clay, pointing. "We shouldn't have any trouble finding it, even though it is a lot farther off than I expected. We must have really gotten off course."

"Let's go," he said.

We practically ran all the way back.

For the rest of the afternoon, Clay and I ignored each other. Finally it was time to pack up the camper and head back to the city.

At my house, Clay threw his things into the back seat of his car, then turned to me.

"Let's stay friends, okay?" he asked. "I know we're not going to be dating anymore, but I still like you."

Ever Mr. Popularity. Besides, there might be more papers that he'd need typed.

"Sure, Clay," I said dryly.

I went into the house and helped B.J. put away the camping gear. When we finished, I fell across my bed with all my clothes on. B.J. watched me from her side of the room. "See? It wasn't such a bad weekend after all, was it?"

I turned my head to look at her. "Not bad? Clay and I broke up and we got lost in the woods and I had to climb a tree to find our way back. Other than that, no, it wasn't such a bad weekend.''

"You broke up?''

"It's definitely over. I think we both knew it was for the best, it's just that neither of us had wanted to be the one to make the first move. I feel completely good about it, so it must have been the right decision.''

"Now what are you going to do? Are you going to tell Paul that you and Clay broke up? I bet he'll be glad to hear it.''

"I don't know if he will or not. Paul's not the kind of guy to wait around for a girl to make all the decisions. I'm afraid I've waited too long.''

Chapter Fourteen

Mrs. Baker put down her pen and her glue brush and turned to me. I was in her advertising office at Jessup's again, where she'd been showing me some future sales notices she'd just gotten in from the main office in Sacramento.

"Marcy," she said to me, "as long as you're this interested in advertising, have you thought about what you're going to do after high school? You'll need some college training if you ever want to advance in this line of work. Just helping out here won't be enough."

"I talked to my school counselor today about taking as many business courses as I can next year, and I plan to take business and advertising in college. I'll be going to San Diego State."

"That's fine. But what about commercial art? Are you at all interested in art?"

"I sure am!" I said. "I've always loved to draw and paint, and I'm pretty good at it. But I never thought of it as a very practical occupation. Whenever I hear about artists it seems that they're always starving. Only a few really make a living at it."

"That's often true. But I'm talking about commercial art. If you're talented, and I suspect you are, it could be very helpful to you in advertising. In fact, it could mean the difference between just having a job and building a career."

"I always thought of my drawing as a hobby."

"Start thinking of it as an opportunity. Look into it, Marcy. You have a chance to do anything you want with your life. Twenty years ago, when I was starting college, the opportunities for women were very limited. Today there is nothing holding you back from becoming whatever you want."

After I left her office I thought hard about what she'd told me. First thing tomorrow morning I would talk to my guidance counselor about the commercial art program at San Diego State.

But right now I wanted to find Paul. I'd hardly seen him in school all day. Every time I tried to catch up with him he seemed to be just a few paces ahead, and moving too fast for me to catch up. I didn't know if he was deliberately avoiding me, and my pride kept me from calling out to him in the school hallways.

Of course everyone knew already that Clay and I had broken up. News like that spread with the speed of a flash flood in our school.

I didn't care. The funny thing was, I'd found that most of the friends I'd made since I'd started dating Clay were still my friends. I knew that at first they'd accepted me mainly because of him, but after I'd gotten to know them and they'd gotten to know me, they had accepted me for myself. A couple of the girls were no longer interested in me now that I no longer had Clay as a status symbol, but I just figured they weren't the type of girls I wanted for friends anyway.

I roamed around Jessup's for a little while, pretending to shop but actually looking for Paul.

"Lose something?" a voice close to my ear said.

I jumped and turned around to see Paul grinning at me. He'd come up behind me. Everything I'd rehearsed carefully in my mind was gone. I just looked at him, like a real airhead.

"I was doing a little shopping," I finally said. "No, that's not true. I was looking for you."

"For me?"

"I haven't seen much of you lately. Even in school I can never seem to catch up with you."

"I had the impression Clay was keeping you pretty busy these days."

"Then you haven't heard—"

"Yes, I heard," he interrupted. "You and Clay broke up."

He wasn't making this very easy for me. I wanted to talk to him, but the middle of a busy department store wasn't the best place.

"What time do you get off work tonight?" I asked.

"I'm off now. On Mondays I only have to come in for a couple of hours after school to help in the stockroom. It's on the weekends that

I get the longer hours." Then he seemed to soften a little bit. "Do you want a ride home?"

I accepted his offer, and a few minutes later we were in his car.

"By the way," he said, "I made it a special point to look at Saturday's ad. Mrs. Baker said you did most of it. It looks good."

"I really only did a little bit of it, but thanks. I was pretty excited to see it."

We talked a little about the ad, and before I knew it, Paul was pulling up at the curb in front of my house.

"Paul—"

"I've got to run, Marcy," Paul said at the same time. "My mother is anxious to get this new lens she ordered." He patted a small square package that rested on the front seat between us. "She kind of relies on me now."

Still without having my say, I climbed out of the car and went inside.

B.J. was home alone, with only Butter to keep her company.

"Holy cow," she said when she saw my face. "If one more thing goes wrong today, I think I'll just lock myself in the bathroom and not come out until everything goes back to normal. Dad went over to Grandma's house because she has a basement full of water and she doesn't trust anyone but him to fix it, and Mom has some sort of crisis at work and will be there most of the evening. Now you come in with your face all droopy looking. What is it, a full moon or something?''

"Paul gave me a ride home.'' I sat down on Dad's recliner and kicked my shoes off. "I wanted to tell him how I felt, but I didn't. I can figure out in my head exactly what I want to say, but the words never made it to my mouth. Paul knows that Clay and I broke up but he acts as though he and I are nothing more than friends.''

"You want my advice?'' B.J. asked.

"Of course I do. That's why I'm telling you all this.''

"Well, it's just that in the past whenever I tried to talk to you about personal stuff like this you always called me a nosy little kid and told me to mind my own business.''

"I did?''

"Yeah. You'd spend hours on the phone talking to Daphne, then you'd walk right past me like I was the invisible woman. It used to really hurt my feelings. Like last year, when Grandma was in the hospital and we thought she might die. Mom and Dad were at the hospital a lot so we were home alone, and you had Daphne come over and spend the weekend to keep you company. But I was scared about Grandma, too, and I couldn't figure out why you needed Daphne when you had me here."

"I never meant to hurt your feelings, B.J. I just never thought you'd understand my problems. So I ignored you. I'm sorry." I thought about what I'd just said. "Lately I've been talking to you about everything, and I know you understand. Funny, but Daphne and I just don't seem to be on the same wavelength anymore. We've both changed, and unfortunately we've gone off in two different directions. A year ago I thought we'd be best friends forever, but now I can hardly talk to her. And we didn't even have a fight or anything like that. We just drifted apart."

The situation with Daphne had been bothering me lately, but until just now I hadn't actually known what the problem was. Putting it into words for B.J. had helped me understand it myself. Daphne and I had changed. It was as simple as that. We no longer considered the same things important.

At the same time B.J. and I had grown closer. I never would have believed it possible to have a little sister as a best friend, but that was exactly what B.J. had become.

"You said something about advice?" I asked, turning to her.

"Yeah. Call Paul up. Sometimes it's easier to say what you're feeling over the telephone."

It made sense, but when I dialed Paul's number I got a busy signal. Then it got to be too late to call and I was forced to wait.

I'd just have to see him in school the next day.

Chapter Fifteen

I sat in Mr. Kirkpatrick's economics class and looked down at the halfway evaluation he'd given on our class experiment. So far he was pleased with the work Paul and I had done on our project, and he especially noted that the extra initiative Paul had shown throughout the experiment had impressed him. We were sure to get a good grade, probably an A.

We were luckier than a lot of others. Daphne was depressed because, according to the experiment, she and Hank were having some financial problems that they couldn't seem to overcome. Of course it wasn't the actual financial status that Mr. K. graded on. It was how you handled the problems that came your way that he considered important.

Daphne's way of handling the problem was to turn it all over to Hank.

"I don't see anything wrong with letting Hank handle it," she whispered to me from her seat directly in front of mine. "He's better at this sort of thing than I am."

I leaned forward and whispered, "I think Mr. Kirkpatrick wants it to be a joint effort."

"How did you do?" She tried to see what he'd written on my paper, but I covered it with my hand. "Did you get a bunch of praise, the way you usually do from teachers?"

I kept my paper covered. No point in making her feel worse. "Paul deserves most of the credit for our project. He's the one who got us out of trouble."

Daphne turned around, and I took that opportunity to peek behind me. There, at the back of the classroom, Paul was watching me. When he saw me look his way he raised one hand in the thumbs-up signal. He'd seen our good report, also.

I smiled at him, then turned around and faced front.

B.J. had given me a ton of encouragement that morning as we were getting ready for school, and I tried to hang on to that now that the moment of truth was arriving.

"Above all, don't be nervous," B.J. had told me. "I know Paul likes you, but if you grovel it might turn him off."

I'd put down my hairbrush and looked at her. "I *never* grovel."

"That's the spirit. Just walk right up to him and say, 'Paul, I'm crazy about you and I think we can make beautiful music together.'"

I'd laughed, which was exactly what she'd wanted. Her joking helped break some of the tension.

After school, I waited for Paul beside his car in the parking lot. I wasn't going to let him get away before I had a chance to talk to him.

"Hi," I greeted him when he finally appeared.

He grinned. "We've got to stop meeting like this." He balanced his books on the roof of the car while he unlocked the door. "We did okay on the economics evaluation, huh?"

"Better than okay," I said, "and most of the credit goes to you."

"It takes two." He retrieved his books. "I have to admit, this whole project has been so much fun that it's hardly seemed like work."

"It's been fun for me, too," I told him.

"Even though you didn't want me for your partner at first?"

"How'd you know that? Did Daphne tell you? I'll kill her if she did!"

"No, Daphne didn't tell me. I was waiting for you outside the classroom that first day, remember? I heard you asking Mr. K. if he would pair you up with someone else."

"Oh, I feel terrible about that!" I said too loudly.

A couple of kids looked at us curiously as they walked past. "I didn't want to hurt your feelings. Besides, I've never regretted the way it turned out. You've been a great partner."

"Thanks." He smiled at me, then looked around the fast-emptying lot. "Well, better shove off."

"Paul, wait." I put a hand on his arm. "I want to tell you something."

He hesitated a moment.

It was now or never.

I looked into those eyes that had fascinated me from day one. He was staring right back at me.

I took a shaky breath. "Paul—"

He stopped me by lightly brushing his fingers across my lips. "I know," he said.

I took his fingers in mine and held on to them.

"You just told me that I'd been a great partner," he said. "How'd you like to be partners for real?"

"It's a deal," I said. "Starting when?"

"What's wrong with right now," he said, making his move.

It was just what I'd had in mind.

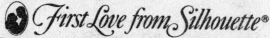

QUANTITY	BOOK #	ISBN #	TITLE	AUTHOR	PRICE
☐	129	06129-3	The Ghost of Gamma Rho	Elaine Harper	$1.95
☐	130	06130-7	Nightshade	Jesse Osborne	1.95
☐	131	06131-5	Waiting for Amanda	Cheryl Zach	1.95
☐	132	06132-3	The Candy Papers	Helen Cavanagh	1.95
☐	133	06133-1	Manhattan Melody	Marilyn Youngblood	1.95
☐	134	06134-X	Killebrew's Daughter	Janice Harrell	1.95
☐	135	06135-8	Bid for Romance	Dorothy Francis	1.95
☐	136	06136-6	The Shadow Knows	Becky Stewart	1.95
☐	137	06137-4	Lover's Lake	Elaine Harper	1.95
☐	138	06138-2	In the Money	Beverly Sommers	1.95
☐	139	06139-0	Breaking Away	Josephine Wunsch	1.95
☐	141	06141-2	I Love You More Than Chocolate	Frances Hurley Grimes	1.95
☐	142	06142-0	The Wilder Special	Rose Bayner	1.95
☐	143	06143-9	Hungarian Rhapsody	Marilyn Youngblood	1.95
☐	144	06144-7	Country Boy	Joyce McGill	1.95
☐	145	06145-5	Janine	Elaine Harper	1.95
☐	146	06146-3	Call Back Yesterday	Doreen Owens Malek	1.95
☐	147	06147-1	Why Me?	Beverly Sommers	1.95
☐	149	06149-8	Off the Hook	Rose Bayner	1.95
☐	150	06150-1	The Heartbreak of Haltom High	Dawn Kingsbury	1.95
☐	151	06151-X	Against the Odds	Andrea Marshall	1.95
☐	152	06152-8	On the Road Again	Miriam Morton	1.95
☐	159	06159-5	Sugar 'n' Spice	Janice Harrell	1.95
☐	160	06160-9	The Other Langley Girl	Joyce McGill	1.95

Your Order Total $_____

☐ (Minimum 2 Book Order)
New York and Arizona residents
add appropriate sales tax $_____

Postage and Handling   .75

I enclose   _____

Name_____

Address_____

City_____

State/Prov._____ Zip/Postal Code_____

First Love from Silhouette

DON'T MISS THESE FOUR TITLES— AVAILABLE THIS MONTH . . .

MAYHEM AND MAGIC Nicole Hart
A Hart Mystery
When May took on a summer job, she found herself involved in a murder attempt. Fortunately she had busybody Eustice and a new attractive boyfriend to help her crack the case.

SOAP OPERA Joyce McGill
Leslie found herself in hot water when she deceived her parents and her new boyfriend in order to get a job as a shampoo girl in a beauty parlor. What would she do when her bubble burst?

PLAYING HOUSE Jean Simon
Now that she was juggling two boyfriends, Marcy should have been having a blast. Yet somehow things had gone awry. How could she have ever thought guys so great?

HUNTER'S MOON Brenda Cole
When Adam showed up with a starved stray at her father's kennels, Katie thought that he was the most attractive boy she'd ever seen. Unfortunately, she was not the first to have felt this way.

WATCH FOR THESE TITLES FROM FIRST LOVE COMING NEXT MONTH

WITH LOVE FROM ROME
Janice Harrell

Was Pine Falls High ready for Wyndham Guiseppi Andrea Sarto, the handsome young Italian heir to the huge Sarto Automobile fortune? More importantly, was Jessica? Are you?

A WISH TOO SOON
Lainey Campbell

Teresa had made up her mind to shake off the dust of boring old Jacksonville and head for the bright lights of the big city. How in the world could she persuade her parents to let her go?

SHADOWS ON THE MOUNTAIN
Miriam Morton

The summer Keni spent in the Smoky Mountains turned out to be the most interesting summer she ever had. It included beautiful scenery, a gorgeous new boyfriend and even a brush with the supernatural.

DOUBLE DARE
Laurien Berenson

After many years of competing in horse shows, Alex learned that there are some things even more important that winning—for example, sharing and loving.

First Love from Silhouette